The Ordeal
of Hogue Bynell

Fic

The Ordeal
of Hogue Bynell

FRANK RODERUS

DOUBLEDAY & COMPANY, INC.

GARDEN CITY, NEW YORK

1982

All the characters in this book
are fictitious, and any resemblance
to actual persons, living or dead,
is purely coincidental.

Library of Congress Cataloging in Publication Data

Roderus, Frank.
The ordeal of Hogue Bynell.

I. Title.
PS3568.O34O7 1982   813'.54
ISBN 0-385-18029-2
Library of Congress Catalog Card Number 82–45303

First Edition
C.) 9/82 Direct 12.00

For Jim and Alma Bronesky

*The Ordeal
of Hogue Bynell*

CHAPTER 1

He heard them coming when they still were some rods distant, heard the clop of shod hoofs and the rattle of bit chains and the faint sounds of good-natured cussing and joking. Hogue Bynell heard them, and his mouth turned down at the corners in a sour grimace. He did not bother to look to see who it was this time—some of them stopped by every month or two weeks in spite of all the time that had passed—but reached instead for the bottle that sat on his desk. He took the bottle, protectively twisted the cork to make sure it was well seated and shoved the nearly full jug into a bottom drawer. He did not feel all that hospitable.

He heard the clatter of iron on rock as the ponies crossed the ballast stone of the roadbed, and a moment later they were beside the shack, tying their animals to the hitch rail there.

The railroad had not installed the rail. It was nonstandard equipment for a relay station out in the middle of the big nothing that stretched from the easternmost escarpments of the Rocky Mountains very nearly the entire distance to Kansas City. Nothing, that is, unless you fancied grass and the livestock that eat it. For a stockman the country was as close to heaven as he ever might expect to get; to an eastern eye it would be a bleak land indeed. Hogue Bynell did not find it at all bleak.

The hitching rail where the cowhands were tying their horses had been erected by a group of Y Knot hands—the brand was stamped:

Y⅁

and required a special iron to burn; it was also about as close as a man could come to being secure from overburns—one Saturday evening when they got tired of passing freights spooking ground-hitched horses.

Hogue shook his head. That had been . . . nearly a year ago now. It seemed incredible that so much time could have passed already. That he had been here so long already. Absolutely incredible.

He heard the clump of bootheels on the platform that lay between his shack and the tracks a few yards distant. A high-pitched ting and tinkle of spur rowels accompanied the footsteps, and the men reached the open door.

They came in without invitation—it would have occurred to none of them that one might be required—and two unshaven faces split apart into hairy grins. The third man, whom Hogue did not know, hung back by the doorjamb with a carefully blank expression, intent on the business of loading a pipe until he saw what their reception might be in this alien environment. Cowhands and railroad men rarely found ground for common meeting.

"Hog! How the hell are you?"

"You ain't changed since the last time we was here, Hog." There was a snort and a loud ring of laughter. "Nope. Ain't shaved and ain't bathed neither. You haven't changed a bit."

"Afternoon, Jimmy, Goodnight," Hogue greeted. Jimmy Lewis was the first who had spoken. Goodnight Licken was the second. Hogue might have heard the man's real first name once, but if so he had forgotten it; Licken had used to work for Mr. Charles Goodnight, down in Texas, and when he first came North talked so much about the legendary cowman that Goodnight had become a nickname that he still wore. Hogue shifted his chin more or less toward the man who still stood in the doorway. "Who's dumb enough to ride beside you two?" It was as close to a polite request for an introduction as Hogue Bynell was likely to get.

"Pete Morris, that there's the Hog," Jimmy said. Which was as close to a formal introduction as he was likely to give.

"Watch out for him," Goodnight added. "He can whip more men, drink more likker, love more women an' eat more chuck than any other three men you ever seen. He don't look like much, but underneath that gentlemanly exterior he's pure hell."

The compliment, and from Goodnight Licken it *was* a compliment, was delivered in a tone of pure friendship, but Hogue Bynell scowled in response. The boys would accept the scowl as a form of modest denial. In fact it was intended to hide the pain that Licken's words had caused. It had been a long, long time since Hogue Bynell had fought with a man or made love to a woman or even cared that much about the food that was required to stoke his body. As for the liquor, well, he still had that. If nothing else he did still have that.

"Sit down if you're so ignorant you can't think of anything better to do," he said.

The boys, this time with the newcomer stepping away from the door and joining them, unstacked some discarded spike kegs that Hogue kept in a corner of the shack for occasional use as chairs. They sat on the upended kegs near the standard-issue potbelly stove by habit, although at this warm time of year the cast-iron stove was covered with a layer of protective grease. There was a bucket of dirt on the floor beside the stove where they could spit, and the iron door was open to receive spent matches and other burnable bits and pieces of trash. In a few more months the summer's accumulation of crud would be done away with in the first fire of the coming fall. The new man, Morris, as lanky and unkempt as the others, lighted his pipe and made use of the opening to dispose of his match.

"You boys ought to be ashamed of yourselves," Hogue ventured, "taking a man's pay and laying off on him like this." He swiveled his chair around and thought wistfully about the bottle hidden in his desk drawer. If he brought it out, he knew, it would only encourage his guests to stay all the longer. He wished they would go away.

"Huh!" Goodnight said with a loud snort. "You're one to talk. Set there behind that hunk o' wood all the day long. Laze around. An' draw pay for it too."

"I can't argue," Hogue said. "It's a fact." He tried to keep the bitterness out of his voice, tried to make it sound light and easy. He was not sure if he had managed that or not.

He must have done all right, he decided. The others were chuckling happily.

Damn fools, he thought. Didn't know when they were well off. Didn't appreciate what they had. Just being able to go out there and snatch their cinches tight and set off at a lope for the camp and a good meal. That should be enough to satisfy any man. It would have satisfied Hogue Bynell well enough. They didn't know when they were well off.

Goodnight pulled a folder of papers from his vest pocket and began to build himself a smoke. Predictably enough,

Jimmy borrowed the makings from him. In a few minutes all three were sitting with their legs crossed and smoke curling around their ears. As content, Hogue thought, as if they had good sense.

They began to talk. About inconsequential things. About the weather and the state of this water hole or that. About a haying crew being sent to Sandy Bottom Run. About that same old brindle cow—you remember her, Hog, the one with the lop ears an' the crookedy left horn—that was gaunted and looked too poor to be worth shooting but which hadn't missed calving once in eleven years now and was the talk of the countryside because of it.

They did not realize it, but each reminiscence, each reference to a remembered watering spot or to that old cow—she had caught Hogue afoot once, when he had stepped off his horse to free a calf mired in thick, gooey mud, and bowled him over with a hooking horn that could have speared him but instead only sent him flying, with bruises to nurse for the next week or so—brought a fresh stab of misery into Hogue's gut.

He remembered the places and the things they were discussing. All too well he remembered them.

Jimmy and Goodnight and the new man chattered on, and Hogue Bynell sat listening in silence, wishing they would go away but unwilling—he did not know himself why it should be so—to send them away.

Hogue sat silently with his ears tuned unwillingly to the conversation that filled the crude, trackside shack, and for a few minutes there he felt a vague sense of embarrassment at what these men were seeing across the standard-issue railroad desk.

Loss of interest in food had caused the fat and even much of the muscle to slough away from what had been a huge and powerful body. He must look shrunken to them now, he thought. His shoulders had thinned and had developed a slope that never used to be there, and his jowls sagged, where once he had been quite moonfaced. His dark brown hair was overly long (he had been whacking at it with shears from time to time but knew he did a poor job of barbering) and had not been brushed in the months since he had last been to town. His eyes remained the deep blue that Jimmy and Goodnight might remember from before, but they no longer had the sparkle and the clarity of robust good health, and the whites were dulled by alcohol and disinterest.

If he stood—which he did not want to do, no matter how long they chose to stay—he would be the same six-foot-three as before. But that would be about all that was unchanged. His weight. . . . He could not really guess what it would be now. He had been something over two-forty in the past. Now. . . . He had no idea and did not particularly want to know.

Hogue sighed. The boys were chattering on, directing their talk to him but not really expecting him to participate. They probably thought they were doing him a favor. He did not think so. Tonight, as always when they came to visit, he would have nightmares again. And that bottle in his desk drawer—he wondered if they knew about it—would be empty before he even began his futile attempts to sleep.

Still, he could not hate them or even dislike them. They had no way of knowing. He sat and listened to the things they had seen and the things they had done in the past few weeks. The wrecks and the blow-ups, which horses had unseated which riders at which morning rope-outs, who had gotten a heavy serving ladle thrown at him when he incurred the cook's wrath . . . and how he had managed to accomplish that easy-to-do feat but had been unfortunate enough to be caught at it.

Tales like those had once been part and parcel of everyday life for Hogue. Now they were so many knives thrown straight to the pit of his stomach.

The visit dragged on for—not hours; Hogue checked the bulky pocket watch the railroad had issued to him—for nearly an hour, although it seemed like more, until Jimmy and Goodnight and Morris rose together as if some signal had been passed between them.

"Reckon we been here long enough to ruin your afternoon nap," Goodnight said. "That's what we really came for, y' know." He chuckled. "Can't let you get away with more'n we can."

There was some good-natured cussing and more than a few lewd jokes, and the three were gone.

"We'll tell you about some of the things that ol' boy done in his time with the Y Knot." Hogue heard Jimmy's voice, pitched low but not quite low enough, as they snugged their cinches and mounted on the far side of the flimsy wall that was Hogue Bynell's protection from summer heat and bitter winter winds alike.

Hogue winced.

He could remember those stories all too well himself.

When they were gone, when the ponies had been mounted and their hoofs had once again rattled across the ballast of the roadbed, Hogue sighed and reached into the drawer for his bottle.

The clickety-tick of an incoming message interrupted him, and almost without conscious thought he reached for his message pad and a pencil. The letters flowed from the telegraph machine onto the paper with hardly any need for a translation stop inside Hogue's brain—it had not always been like that; he used to have to work at it, but now it was so automatic he scarcely had to think about a relationship between what he was hearing and what he was writing—and the routine train order was ready for posting.

Hogue tore the order from the pad and rolled it into a pickup pouch.

As automatically as he had accepted and receipted for the train order, Hogue reached for his crutches and clumped his way out onto the platform to rig the pouch for a flying pickup by the midday eastbound.

He stood with a crutch under each arm, a tall, gaunt figure of what once had been a huge and powerful man. But now he was only large and—he suspected—pathetic to see. The right leg of his sturdy broadcloth trousers had been cut off and neatly pinned beneath the stump that ended ten inches below his right hip.

The doctors had told him that he would come to accept the loss of the leg as normal, that he would adjust to it to the point that he would scarcely miss the lost limb.

The doctors had been wrong.

CHAPTER 2

It had been a good life while it lasted. The dreams of open country and a free life had begun in the sweat and grime of a Missouri farm and become realized in South Texas and along the long trails that led from Texas across the Indian Nations to the raucous railheads of Kansas.

Hogue Bynell had become a hand. He thought of himself as a top hand, and sometimes he had even drawn pay on that elite basis.

He took to the life of a cowhand with the enthusiasm of a young lover in the midst of his first affair. The grinding monotony of long hours and foul weather and unrelenting labor of the trail drovers could not begin to blunt his eagerness.

He learned to wear his hat brims wider and his boots tighter than any city dweller would deem remotely acceptable, and when he went into a town—any town, because they all came to look alike to him—he wore his gloves with their fancily embroidered attached gauntlets tucked under his belt as a badge of office, a clear statement to any who cared to look that this man was a cowhand and therefore was not to be trifled with.

He learned that money was for blowouts and good times, that as long as a man owned a saddle, a pair of spurs and a good name he was a free man. And in the big-grass country a good name had nothing to do with morality, geniality or any

of the other, "normal" yardsticks used to measure character
inside town limits. On the big grass a good name came from
knowledge of cows and horses and a willingness to do the
work. Beyond that, character was a personal and private matter, of interest only to the individual and to those he might
choose to annoy.

Hogue Bynell liked the way of life. Given the choice, he
would have continued in it indefinitely. He had not been
given that choice.

He had come to the Y Knot outfit, which ranged from
Cheyenne Wells south to the dry lands below the Arkansas
and from east of Pueblo very nearly to the Kansas border,
some five years before. He had to do considerable thinking to
reach that figure. He tended to remember the years by seasons and shippings and droughts, rather than by any numeri-
cal designations.

The Y Knot crew had been a good one, the work neither
easier nor more difficult than it would have been anywhere
else. The only thing that really distinguished it was that there
was no brush to buck here and the roping was easier. Hogue
had taken a look around at a country where a man could ride
for days and see nothing but grass and beef and an occasional
rock, and he had declared himself at home. He sold his
chaps, unnecessary in country where there were no thorns to
be fended away from the legs, to a wide-eyed kid signing on
for his first job, and Hogue settled in to stay. Or so he
thought.

In addition to grass, grazing livestock and rocks there was
one other feature common to the open plains.

Dry washes and jagged arroyos crossed the nearly flat land
here and there, running water at only the rarest of times,

sandy nearly always. They did not carry nearly enough water for their presence to be marked by tree lines or the growth of brush along their banks.

On a dreary afternoon in March with the ground still greasy with melting subsoil ice, Hogue had dabbed his rope onto a feisty, crossbred steer that had broken a horn and needed doctoring. It was something Hogue had done in the past more times than he could remember even if he had had a reason to try to count them all. It was part of the everyday work, and he thought not a thing of it.

The steer had resisted the rope, as was a steer's God-given right if not exactly a steer's natural duty, and Hogue's horse had gone about the business of teaching the cantankerous bovine who was the boss and who the bossee.

As a student of the Texas cowmen, Hogue Bynell was a tie-fast roper just as naturally as a California or Oregon buckeroo was a dally man. The free end of Hogue's rope was tied hard and fast to his saddle horn on the day the rope was cut from the bale to be stretched and rubbed, and it was not removed from the horn until the day it was replaced. That was the way Hogue and a thousand others like him had been taught to do it and that was the way he would continue to do it for as long as he could hold a coil of hemp in his hands, plain and simple. There was no other way to work.

This time, though, the steer put up a fight that would not have shamed a Mexican black bull, of which Hogue had roped at least his share in the past. It was an effort that was exceptional for a crossbred northern steer but nothing Hogue had not handled many times before. If anything the challenge was an unexpected pleasure.

The fight went awry when the tight-pulled hemp of

Hogue's rope scraped across the already painfully sensitive stub of the steer's broken horn. A gout of fresh blood sprayed from the new damage, splattering the steer's near shoulder with bright red blotches and sending the half ton of frightened animal into a frenzy of motion.

Hogue's horse slipped on the poor footing caused by the melting ice in the soil and very nearly fell. Hogue, securely locked in the saddle, thought the whole fight delightful. He automatically shifted his weight with the movements of the horse beneath him and laughed out loud.

The horse righted itself and backed away from a sudden charge of the steer, scrambling to the rear to regain tension on the rope, as he had been taught in the hard school of cow work.

But behind the horse was the sharp-cut bank of one of those countless, nameless dry washes, unnoticed in the midst of the fight that had been going on, and the horse's back legs reached the edge before Hogue could spot the danger and spur the animal ahead.

Again the greasy footing displayed its treachery, and when the horse, a solid, heavy-bodied sorrel, tried to scramble out of danger, its feet slipped over the edge, and horse and man plunged backward for half a dozen feet to the pea gravel and hard sand of the wash bottom.

Hogue tried to jump clear, but the toe of his boot hung up for a fraction of a second in the stirrup—tapaderos were no longer in fashion, he reflected time and time again afterward, or the accident likely could not have occurred—and he was able to throw himself only partially clear of the falling body.

Horse and man landed together, and Hogue was able to distinctly hear the crack of a bone snapping in two. It sounded very much like a half-dried limb being broken into firewood-size pieces. At the time, Hogue was hoping it was one of his own bones that he heard break, rather than the horse's. His bones would knit—they had had to often enough before—and the sorrel was one of the best circle horses he had ever had in his string.

He got his wish. The bone was his.

The horse rolled, came to its feet and shook itself like a dog before it trotted a few steps away and stood with its reins dangling, waiting for instructions from the man who was its master. The rope that had been tied to the injured steer was dangling also. The immense pressures applied by the sudden fall had broken the three-eighths hank of fibers, and the steer was long gone.

Hogue knew that he was hurt, but he was not particularly alarmed. He had been hurt before. The pain was somewhat more extreme this time than before, but a man could not ask for everything. He had not done anything really stupid, like breaking his neck. It was only a leg. Again.

Experience told him there was no point in trying to straighten it alone. He set his teeth against the pain, deliberately decided against looking under his jeans to see the damage that had been done, and began crawling toward the waiting horse.

He made it to the sorrel and pulled himself hand over hand up the stirrup leathers to the saddle.

Getting his injured right leg over the cantle was a bit of a problem, but eventually he managed it. He did some fancy cursing along the way, and if there had been anyone around to hear and record his words he might well have found a niche in local history for the broad range and choice selections of his invective. As it was, his talents went unrecognized.

He made a mental note of where the steer had last been seen. Someone else would have to come out and finish the job or the wound might fester and $32 worth of beef on the hoof be lost to the owners of the Y Knot. Then he rode slowly back to the camp they were using for this early-spring working.

The cook cut his jeans off him—which Hogue deeply resented; the trousers had cost $2 at the next-to-the-nearest store they could reach or $2.15 at the nearest—and announced that the break would heal in time but that they would have to coat the injury with hot pine tar to avoid putrefaction. The jagged end of a broken bone had come through the skin.

Hogue did not look forward to the burn of the tar, but he was not particularly worried. This was not the humid Gulf Coast, where wounds festered easily. This was the dry, high plains, and here man and animal were mostly free of that problem. Here a wound healed quick and clean.

The cook attended to his duties, and the boys, including Goodnight and Jimmy, ribbed him for his carelessness and stupidity, and Hogue began making plans about what kind of hell he could raise from a horizontal position the next time the supply wagon rolled into town. There were several selections to choose from in that planning, and Hogue ultimately decided to reject none of them. It surely would take long enough for the leg to heal that he would be able to try them all. If his money held out.

The wagon would not be going to town again for another

ten days or so, so he had plenty of time to anticipate the various pleasures he planned.

By the third day of Hogue's enforced indolence, the cook and the camp boss were beginning to look worried about something.

By the fifth day, Hogue was beginning to work his nostrils and wonder what the ugly smell was that was bothering him.

On the sixth day, the cook tried to undo the too-obvious damage with a Y Knot branding iron heated beyond the dull gray that marks a properly fired iron to the cherry red that is used for cauterization.

On the seventh day, the camp boss admitted that he had made a mistake and dispatched Hogue in the camp wagon on a jolting trip to town.

There a doctor who claimed extensive wartime experience with just such cases shook his head in response to all of Hogue's protests, gave the injured cowboy a bottle of bonded rye to suck on and prepared his knives and saws for use.

The gangrene had already gone too far, the doctor said stubbornly. The leg came off or its owner died, and Hogue was not going to be given the choice. When Hogue demurred, someone shoved a nasty-smelling fold of gauze under his nose, and that was the end of the argument.

When Hogue came to again, there was only an expanse of flat-lying sheet where his right leg should have been and another bottle of rye on the bedstand to help him ease the pain.

That had been just over two years ago now. It had been that long since Hogue Bynell sat on a horse or held a rope in his hand. Or thought of himself as a man.

In the meantime he had had to find work. He had given it a great deal of thought before he arrived at his decision.

He could have clerked in a store or done some sort of menial make-work, but the thought of being in a town where people would see him and point at his back all day every day was intolerable.

Being a sheepherder would have been all right. They practically never had to look at another human or be looked at by one. But a one-legged man could not chase woolies any more than he could work cows, even if damned sheepherders only did wear one spur. So that was out.

Finally he decided on the railroad. A telegraph operator could do his work sitting down, and the railroads were always looking for fools who would be willing to endure the lonely isolation of a relay station. Hogue even had one in mind, out on the big grass where there was nothing but a shack and a set of shipping pens that was used twice a year.

Hogue Bynell was not a stupid man. He was capable of learning, once he set his mind to it.

He set his mind to the problem of learning to interpret clicks and clacks and make them come out as letters, and when he was satisfied with his own proficiency he crutched his way into the trainmaster's office in Pueblo and told the bossman he was ready to go to work.

The bossman was impressed, not so much by Hogue's proficiency, which was undeniable, as by the fact that this one-legged stranger made no mention of either pay or relief time in his request for a job that no one else wanted. Relay Station 12 was a problem post and always had been.

Hogue spent a month, without pay, learning the line's peculiar way of doing things and then became the line's lowest-paid telegraph relay operator.

He had been there ever since.

He intended to remain exactly there for as long as he had the strength to fist a key and enough hearing to read the dots and dashes.

A man cannot ask for everything. Hogue Bynell asked for nothing. Except possibly to be left alone.

That would be quite enough right there.

CHAPTER 3

The actual work at the relay station was not enough to keep a man busy, which probably caused no end of complaint for the sharp-penciled accountants who had to justify the pay that Hogue Bynell and other operators like him drew from the line, however little that might have been.

The MK&C was neither the busiest nor the most prosperous of lines. But it made do.

The route ran from an eastern terminus at Kansas City, Missouri, through central Kansas, into Colorado north of the Arkansas River Valley to a western terminus at Pueblo. The country served was mostly grass, the freight mostly beef on the hoof. The eastern third of the line also hauled grain and served farm communities with their freight needs, but there was relatively little traffic on the western two thirds of the line.

Four regularly scheduled freights, each with a single passenger car attached but sparsely occupied, passed Relay Station 12 daily. Specials would shuttle back and forth perhaps three times weekly for one reason or another.

Bynell's job was to receive and relay train orders from the trainmaster in Pueblo to the engineers on the steam-driven, coal-fired locomotives. The appearance of a special anywhere on the line would require one train or another to shunt onto a siding until the other was safely by on the single set of through tracks. Railroads tend to frown on collisions, and freights are not noted for any quick-stop abilities. It was Hogue's job and that of the other operators like him to ensure that no accidents occurred.

In the year and a half since Hogue had taken over his post on the big grass there had been no accidents on his stretch of the line, nor were there any near misses.

The work was essentially mechanical and untrying, and the trainmaster—who had a reputation of being mechanical and without humor—had come to accept the Relay 12 operator as one of the machines under the master's care. Perhaps more reliable than most pieces of mechanized equipment but a machine nonetheless.

Once each week a work train routinely stopped at Relay 12 to deliver groceries, clothing, liquor or whatever else Hogue had submitted on his weekly shopping list. The actual buying was done in Pueblo by an office boy, and the amount spent each week was carefully tabulated and deducted from Bynell's pay. A relay operator was given a roof and a bed out of the generosity of the line. Anything beyond that was his own responsibility.

Hogue's primary expense was for liquor—locally bottled bar whiskey. He did not feel he could afford bonded liquor although in fact he never had any idea of how much money he might have riding on the company books; he had drawn cash from the line on only three occasions, when he chose to take relief time in town, and each of those times he had regretted leaving the station. His food bill was very small. As he neither went anywhere nor had anyone around who would have to smell him on a regular basis, he required practically nothing in the way of soap and clothing.

Having little to do during his waking hours except to stay awake and listen for the clatter of the telegraph key, Hogue spent most of his time carving lumps of coal into cunningly crafted horses, steer heads, saddles, jackrabbits or anything else that came to mind. He sculptured from memory but was becoming more than barely proficient at the exercise. There being no market that he knew of for such homemade time wasters, he burned the pieces in his little cooking stove on those few occasions when he got around to eating.

A few of the crewmen from the regular work trains knew about his pastime, and once one of them had asked him to carve a "horsie" for his daughter to play with. The brakeman offered to supply Hogue with wood for the carving and to pay him a dime for his efforts. The request was not repeated. Hogue threw an almost empty bottle at the man and just missed his head. At it was, the brakeman went home that night reeking of spilt whiskey and caught the Holy Ned from his churchgoing wife.

As far as Hogue was concerned, he was employed by the railroad but was not necessarily part of it.

The train crews were an inescapable part of his existence on a once-per-week basis, but they were neither friends nor co-workers. They were simply there. They delivered what he had to have and they took away his list for the next week's delivery, and that was that. They were as useful to him as a dependable horse once had been. He had felt more attachment for the horses.

As far as Hogue was concerned, he was *not* a railroad man, he was simply an employee of the line. Hogue Bynell was and intended to remain a cowhand. Down on his luck and out of his proper employment, but a cowhand regardless. The railroad merely served to avoid starvation.

Once each month, the work train also delivered to him a letter.

None of those letters had been answered since the last time Hogue requested a few days of relief and rode the work train back into Pueblo, which was nearly five months now, but the letters addressed to him care of the MK&C continued to arrive, all in the same spidery handwriting. The crewmen on the work train might have wondered about the letters, but none of them ever asked the Relay 12 operator about them, even though the penmanship was unmistakably feminine.

The lady's name was Mabel Cutcheon. *Mrs.* Mabel Cutcheon. Widow of Jonathan C. Cutcheon, of Pueblo, who had run a dry-goods store catering to cowhands and cattlemen until a piece of gristle lodged in his throat had cut him short in the middle of his forty-eighth year.

That had been sometime before Hogue's accident, and the widow had taken immediate aim on the big, sometimes rowdy but always polite cowhand who dealt at Cutcheon's Emporium whenever he was in town.

There had been a time back then when Hogue was almost tempted to allow the widow to succeed in her goal of taking Mr. Bynell to an altar. The lady was not unattractive for her age, was warmhearted and certainly did not have to be paid for the time she spent with him. That was a unique experience for a cowboy who had left home at an early age and who had never before associated with any woman with whom a female choir singer would be seen talking on the street.

The accident had eliminated that temptation. There were

some things that a man simply did not do, and accepting charity from a woman was in that category. It seemed perfectly obvious to Bynell that any continued expressions of interest in him would fall in the same charitable ranking as the adoption of a Mexican brat or the taking in of a stray cur. A one-legged man is not a whole man is not a man, and that was that.

Hogue had some vestiges of pride left, although rather few, he thought, and that one he chose to cling to. As far as he was concerned, the widow Cutcheon was no longer within reach, her protestations to the contrary notwithstanding.

He accepted a few dinners from her after the accident but nothing more than that. When the pressures built within him, until he learned to submerge his baser inclinations in light but regular applications of cheap whiskey, taken internally, he resumed his old habit of seeking out the soiled doves who wore red clothing and rather little of it.

For a time, he had been willing to continue his relationship with the widow on a level of friendship, but his last visit to her home had brought him closer than he wanted to be to temptations that he did not want to acknowledge. He did not want that to happen again and so no longer answered her letters with the long, dull instruments he used to prepare day after day in the isolation of Relay Station 12.

Hogue felt himself much more satisfied with life now than he had been then. He was very nearly entirely disconnected from the world beyond the station walls, and he liked it that way.

If the Y Knot hands would quit coming by to visit, he would like it even better.

And one of these times—soon, he thought—he would get

rid of the small metal box in his desk that held more than a year's accumulation of letters, all of which were signed, "Affectionat'ly y'rs, Mabel."

One of these times.

Until then, Hogue Bynell was doing just fine, thank you. Just fine.

CHAPTER 4

The visitors showed up two days after the Y Knot cowboys had stopped by for their every-so-often chat. Hogue heard them coming when they were still some distance away. He might be a cripple, but there was nothing wrong with his hearing.

When he heard them, he assumed they were more boys from the Y Knot. No one else ever rode here except during the spring and fall shipping seasons, when large crews of hands would be there to crowd the beeves onto specially laid-on trains of cattle cars. But this was not the time of year for that, and anyway he would have received train orders if anyone were shipping off season. So it could not be that.

As always he heard the approach of the horses, but this time they also came from the wrong direction to be from any of the Y Knot camps that Hogue could remember. They came up behind the shack and did not have to cross the tracks to reach the hitching rail.

Odd, he thought. He made a sour face. Two sets of visitors in less than a week were three times as many people as he wanted to see.

They tied their horses at the rail, and a moment later he could hear their boots on the wooden platform. There was no sound of spurs ringing with their steps, which was also odd. Hogue had never heard of a ranch that supplied its men with horses so tame they could be used without loud cussing and hard spurring. It was for sure the Y Knot never laid out the cash for over-gentle animals like that.

When the men reached the doorway, Hogue saw that both of them were total strangers.

Well, they could go as easily as they had come. His jug was hidden in his desk drawer and his crutches were down out of sight along the wall, and the hell with the pair of them.

"This isn't a regular station," he said curtly. "The trains don't stop here and I don't sell no tickets." He ducked his head and pretended to be reading a train-order copy that had already been posted and picked up.

After a moment, he realized that the two men were not leaving, as he had expected, and wanted, them to. He looked up again.

Both continued to stand in the doorway, looking at him. He did not like that. He did not like them. He was no freak in any traveling show to be gawked at by passersby.

The one on the left was of medium height and a hefty build, much as Hogue had used to be, except considerably shorter. The one on the right was the same height give or take an inch and much leaner. Both were bearded and had wide-brimmed hats pulled low over their eyes.

Both were dressed like cowhands. Trousers pegged into their boot tops, vests worn over their flannel shirts, neckerchiefs knotted around their throats and hanging loose. No gloves or gauntlets, but that did not mean anything. Gloves were out of fashion these days and bandannas were in. Sometimes Hogue thought that cowhands were as fashion-conscious as schoolgirls were reputed to be. He felt vaguely disloyal when he had such thoughts, but once in a while they popped into mind in spite of that.

Still, there was something about these two that made Hogue doubt that they were engaged in the husbanding of cattle anyway. Maybe just that they were a bit too clean. A hand cannot work without gathering a layer of horse sweat and horsehair, dried manure and dried dust and dried blood. It simply was not possible, given the work that had to be done.

These two were carrying enough dust on their clothes, but the other ingredients were missing.

Besides, they did not look to him as though they knew or cared all that much about beeves. It was nothing he could put a name to, just an impression.

And he did not care enough about either man to bother examining his impression. He just wanted them to go away and leave him alone.

"I said—"

"We heard you." It was the stocky one, on the left, who had spoken.

Both of them came on through the doorway to stand inside.

Hogue scowled at him. He had become rather good at scowling in the past few years, although he had not had much practice at it before then. They ignored him and looked around the shack.

There was little enough there to require study, Hogue knew.

The front portion of the tiny shack was occupied by the desk and by a broad shelf of instruments and wires. Beneath the shelf were some storage cabinets and the lever to throw the never-used signal flag. Hogue did not even know why they had bothered to install the thing, since no passengers ever entrained here, but it was standard equipment and therefore had to be part of any station that was built.

The back part of the shack held the potbelly stove in the center and beyond it, away from the desk, the smaller cooking stove and the piled spike kegs that sometimes served as chairs. Closer, between the desk and the back wall, there was a rope-sprung bunk. Some pegs over the bunk and a small trunk shoved under it were all the wardrobe Hogue required.

There were no pictures or fancy doodads on the walls. No paint, either, for that matter. Looking at it fresh, which he had not done in more than a year, Hogue would have had to admit that as a home the relay shack was not much. Still, it was all he needed. He certainly did not care what impression it left on visitors.

"We're passing through," the stocky one said. "Thought we'd stay the night here under a roof an' get an early start tomorrow."

"It's early to be stopping," Hogue objected. It was only midafternoon.

The stocky man shrugged. "Our horses are tired. They need the rest."

Hogue gave him a shrug in return. "It's a free country. You can camp where you like."

The stocky man smiled. The expression looked like it did not fit his face. "We'd sure appreciate the loan of your roof. It's been a long time."

Hogue grunted. He was not about to commit herself to an invitation he did not want to give.

"I'm Charles Porter. Everybody calls me Chuck. My saddle

partner here is Alonzo Trapp. You can call him Al. Everybody does."

Hogue managed to restrain himself from uttering expressions of great joy at the acquaintance.

"And what do they call you?" Chuck seemed to be an almighty insistent sort, Hogue thought. But he answered the
man.

"Mighty pleased to meet you, Mr. Hogue. Mighty
pleased."

Hogue corrected him. Chuck smiled apologetically. That
did not look natural on his face either. "Sorry 'bout that,
Hogue. We wouldn't want to give you offense."

Now they were on a first-name basis all around, it seemed.
Hogue was less than thrilled.

The clickety-tap of the electromagnetic receiver gave him
a diversion that he welcomed. He turned away from the odd
pair and began to copy the message, even though the signal
was meant for Relay Station 10, off to the east.

Hogue had never seen Relay 10, or any of the others for
that matter.

For some reason—possibly to impress potential investors—
the relay stations all carried even numbers. There was no Station 11 between Relay 10 and Relay 12. Hogue had met the
operator of Relay 10 when the man passed through for relief
time on the work train. The fellow was thin and mousy and
nervous and in spite of his isolation did not drink. He also
had two good legs and could have been doing something better with his life than sitting in some shack with nothing but
the wind and blowing cinders for company. Hogue did not
like him.

He copied the message verbatim and made a show of filing

it away, although actually he would get around to burning it eventually. When he looked up again, Chuck and Al were still there, but now they had helped themselves to seats on a pair of his kegs.

"I don't have food enough to feed you," Hogue lied. The truth was that he had more than he needed. And if any grub-line riders ever came through he would probably break down and feed them. He had been in that situation a time or two himself in the past. But these two did not look as though they were grub-line riders, and neither looked underfed.

"That's all right," Chuck said. "We have aplenty of our own. Don't want to put you out any. We just want to rest our horses and borry your roof for a while. That's all."

Hogue grunted again. He could not think of much he might say that would dissuade them. The damned men seemed perversely intent on hanging around where they were not wanted. "Suit yourself," he growled.

They did. Chuck and Al—Hogue had already forgotten their last names—sat as content as a pair of dead clams and whispered to each other, dirtying Hogue's plank flooring with their cigarette ashes while Hogue pretended to concentrate on papers on his desk.

He copied a few more messages meant for other stations, took down a flimsy for the 5:12 eastbound ordering the engineer to off-track at Antelope Siding until a westbound special freight cleared, and rolled the train order into its pouch. He laid the filled pouch on the edge of his desk and deliberately procrastinated for a while. He had plenty of time before he had to hang the pouch on the hook for the flying pickup.

There had been a good many westbound specials lately, he reflected. Probably because of the mining activity up in the mountains. The Denver and Rio Grande had been carrying freight up there for some time, but generally connections with it were made from the east by way of the Union Pacific and Julesburg. Now there was some new little outfit open: the Florence and Victor or some such name. And there was a good bit more traffic on the MK&C to connect with it. If Hogue cared anything about the railroad he would probably find that gratifying, but he did not.

Still, thinking about it gave him another distraction from the unwelcome presence in the shack.

The two men were ignoring him as completely as he was ignoring them, though. That was something to be pleased about. Not much, but something.

An hour ground slowly by, and Hogue began to look at his watch more and more often. Before long he would have no choice.

And eventually he did not. The 5:12 would be along within two minutes of 5:12, plus or minus. The trainmaster would see to that or there would be absolute hell to pay along the line. No one got off schedule on Henry Bertram's track. *No* one.

And it was already approaching five o'clock. The order had to be posted. There was no choice about it.

If Hogue had been feeling irritation before, it had nothing to compare with the mingled frustration and anger he was beginning to feel now.

But there was absolutely no help for it. He had to post the order on the hook. And he had to walk out onto the platform to do that. *Crutch* out there. Like some damned gimp. Which he was, he reminded himself bitterly.

If he had to do it, he would do it. He bent and picked up

his crutches and came nimbly to his full height on the power-ful limb that his one good leg had become. He did not him-self realize how much change there had been in that pre-viously seldom used left leg—a cowhand rarely thinks in terms of walking or running and cares very little about legs except in terms of reaching a saddle—but for some time now Hogue had been able to hop around the inside of the shack without benefit of the crutches without really being aware that he did it as easily as he did.

Now he was conscious mainly of an acute embarrassment as these unwelcome strangers would be treated to the specta-cle of Hogue Bynell, Telegrapher and Chief Cripple.

Bastards, he muttered to himself.

He swung himself forward on the crutches with the ease of long habit and forced himself to not look at his guests. He did not have to look, in any case. He *knew* they were staring at him.

He went out onto the platform and crossed it to trackside, using his goad pole to place the courier pouch onto the hook, where the engineer of the passing train could snag it, and raised the signal flag on its standard to alert the train before it reached the shack. Backing up and making another pass was not easily done with something as ponderous as a railroad train, and woe unto the poor operator or crewman who blew a pickup.

Hogue turned to make his way back inside. Damn them, he told himself. Damn them to hell and back two times. He would buy their round-trip tickets himself if he could.

Both of them, moonfaced Chuck and silent Al, had come to the door to gawk at the cripple while he did his work. They were standing there right now.

If he thought he was man enough to whip them, Hogue thought, he would take a swing at them right now. But with what. A crutch? That would be ludicrous. Instead he gave them an icy glare and swung past them with as much dignity as he could muster.

Hogue went back to his desk and buried himself in work that did not exist. He hoped the two would go away. He just hoped they would go away soon.

CHAPTER 5

Hogue did not need an alarm clock. The eastbound 4:43 took care of that for him. It was odd, really, that that was the only train he ever heard passing. Day or night, the others could rumble past a few feet away from his bunk and he would never hear them. But the 4:43—or the opening ticks of his receiver—would bring him bolt upright from a sound sleep.

As always, Hogue sat up and reached in the semidarkness for his shirt and trousers. Damned annoying, this not being able to put his pants on without the bedside or a chair to sit on, but it was one of the things he had gotten used to. He had learned to keep everything he needed close at hand so he did not have to go awandering in the dark. It had taken him a few nasty tumbles before that became a firm habit.

Leaving his crutches where they were, he hopped first to the can of dirt beside the stove and tried to get rid of some of the previous night's lingering foul taste by spitting. It never worked, but he tried it every morning.

When that failed he hopped to his desk and took a short pull at his bottle. That did help. He felt almost human again.

Hogue shook his shoulders to throw off a morning chill and picked up his crutches. He needed to make his usual morning trek around to the outhouse. For a man on crutches that short jaunt could become quite an adventure on wintry mornings, but he would not have to worry about that for some months to come.

He reached the door and stopped in puzzlement.

Those two men, Chuck and Al—he had to think for a moment to recall their names—were gone.

He had become quite blunt with them the night before, they insisting that they wanted to sleep inside the relay station with a roof over their heads and he insisting just as firmly that they were not going to.

Finally they had made a camp of sorts across the tracks with their horses—exceptionally fine animals, Hogue had seen—tethered to picket pins so they could graze during the night.

Now the site was empty except for a black, barren circle where they had built a fire shortly after nightfall.

Odd behavior, Hogue thought. The two had been so set on staying, so determined that their horses—which Hogue had thought looked to be in fine shape—should be rested.

And now it seemed they had pulled out during the night sometime.

They had not even come inside to get a drink from the water barrel. There was no well or spring at the relay station, so drinking water was hauled by the work train along with other consumables. Hogue knew good and well he could have slept through their breaking camp fifty or sixty yards away. But he would *not* have slept through some stranger's presence inside the shack itself. No way.

So they had picked up and left without even coming in for that. He would not have expected, or wanted, a farewell from the odd pair, but a drink of water . . . that was something else.

He shook his head and looked more closely at the scorched earth where their fire had been.

It was not of enough interest that he would want to bother navigating his crutches through the loose rock ballast under the ties, but from where he stood he could see no hint of smoke or any rise of heat shimmer from coals that should have remained where the fire had been.

That meant the men probably had not stayed long enough to refuel the fire. They must have left shortly after Hogue turned in for the night.

Not that he really cared what they had done. Just as long as they were gone. That was quite enough. Still shaking his head, he continued along the platform and around back on the often used path to the backhouse.

Hogue was carving another lump of coal. Eventually the jagged piece of soft black rock—or whatever the stuff really was, he did not know for sure—would become the head and neck of a pronghorn antelope. Hogue had plenty of life models to work from; all he had to do was walk to the door and nearly as often as not there would be a white-rumped antelope or several within his view. At the moment, the piece resembled only a curiously shaped lump of coal as he began to mold the slightly outcurving line of the neck leading to the throat. Detailing, including small incisions made with the point of his pocketknife to provide hair on the animal's smooth hide, would come later. Right now he was concentrating on a rough shape for the piece.

It was pleasant enough work, and he had nothing else that he needed to do. The early westbound had already roared by, a minute and a half late and making up time. There had been no order on the hook to be picked up, and the engineer had not stopped for coffee and a chat.

The work train always came in the morning hours, but that would not be until. . . . Hogue could not remember if it was two days or three until it was due again. He sometimes lost track of the days of the week, although month, date, and year had to be included on all of his paperwork. That he had to keep up with, the days of the week he did not. The work train came on Fridays.

Another eventless day loomed. Hogue welcomed it. He yawned and began to undercut what would become the powerful jaw line of an adult pronghorn buck.

Damn!

He could hear horses. Again. They were distant, but he was sure of it. A ridden horse has a completely different pattern of beats on the earth from a loose animal. These seemed to be moving at a road jog.

The place seemed to be becoming more popular than the Pueblo terminus the past few days.

Hogue felt angry enough to spit. As it was, he slammed his knife onto the desk top and threw the so-carefully started pronghorn carving into the corner beyond his little cooking stove. The partially worked carving hit the wall and shattered.

The ridden horses moved closer. With any luck, they would ride on by.

They did not.

They came up behind the shack, and Hogue could hear several men tying up at the hitch rail.

Whoever they were, he did not want to see them, but apparently he had no choice. They were crossing the platform.

Then they reached the doorway, and he *really* did not want to see them.

There were three this time. Chuck and Al and a wizened little fellow who was dwarfed by the other two even though neither Chuck nor Al was particularly tall.

The newcomer had a stubble of beard that was obviously sloppy rather than deliberate, and the color of the facial hair was much more white than dark. Streaks of dirty gray ran through the hair on his head, too, along with a liberal accumulation of grease. The man's clothes looked several sizes too large for him, and his boots looked as if they would have been rejected by a besotted Indian.

Even I am not as much of a slob as that, Hogue thought critically.

Not that Hogue was apt to like the man in any event, but this guy was a down-and-out'er of the first water. Hogue wondered if he was a hobo who had gotten drunk and fallen off the rails. Maybe Chuck and Al had picked him up somewhere along the tracks and brought him back here for the railroad to adopt. Maybe that was it.

Well, Hogue Bynell did not need a pet. He was doing just fine without drifters and bums, thank you, and he would tell them exactly that.

He opened his mouth to speak, or perhaps to snarl, but closed it again without a sound.

There was something new about Chuck and Al, too. And he did not particularly like it.

This morning, both men were wearing guns. And while that in itself was not particularly startling in this country, both of them were wearing their iron low with fancy thongs tying the holsters to their thighs.

That was a trick Hogue had seen just twice before in all the years and all the cow towns and trails he had seen, and neither time had the wearer been anything but pure mean.

An honest cowhand wears his gun, if he wants to wear one, which he probably does not to begin with, any old dangling place he can put it or it winds up shifting into.

The big-time gunfighters, and Hogue had seen a couple of those, too, wore their guns in cross-draw or shoulder rigs under their coats. They at least pretended to be gentlemen about an ugly business.

But this tie-down business. That was more likely for creeps who thought they were something special. And that kind of idiot Hogue Bynell or any other halfway sensible human person ought to avoid.

Hogue noticed too that gun-toting Chuck and gun-toting Al were not smiling this morning or making any pretense at being friendly.

Both of them, in fact, looked downright serious.

Hogue wondered if they would go quietly away again if he ignored them. Somehow he did not really think they would.

CHAPTER 6

"You weren't all that friendly last night," Chuck said. "We think you owe us a small favor. Sorta to make up for that, if you know what I mean." He was not smiling when he said it. None of them were.

Hogue grunted a noncommittal response. He was reasonably sure he was not going to like whatever this favor turned out to be.

"What it is," Chuck went blandly on, "we'd like you to deliver a message for us on that pickup hook of yours. To the early-afternoon westbound. That's all we want. You do that an' then we go quietly away. Very simple. Nobody bothers nobody else. We get what we want and we ride off down the tracks like we'd never been here. Okay?"

Hogue grunted again. He had a feeling he already knew what the answer would be, more or less, but he asked the question anyway. "What kind of message?"

Chuck grinned. "A siding stop, that's all."

"An unscheduled siding stop, right?"

Chuck shrugged. "You could say that we're making the new schedule. Temporarily."

"And I suppose you know somewhat more than I do about the freight that westbound might be carrying."

There was that grin again. "We got no way of knowing

what it is you know about it, but in case you've figured it out, yeah, there's a payroll on that train."

"And you figure you could use it better than the boys it's intended for," Hogue said.

"Don't worry about it," Chuck said. "The railroad's insured for the loss. An' anyway they could afford it even if they wasn't. It's no skin off your nose."

Al spoke for the first time. As far as Hogue could remember, it was the first time the man had said anything at all directly to him although he had done some low-voiced yammering at his partner the day before. Hogue disliked Chuck in much the same way he disliked nearly everyone he met these days, but that was nothing compared with the way he felt about Al.

"It'll be plenty skin off you if you don't do what we say," Al said.

The three of them moved on inside the shack and began helping themselves to seats on the spike kegs he had not yet gotten around to replacing in the corner where he usually stored them. The newcomer had to fetch a third one off the pile and seemed to be having difficulty handling it. Whoever he was he still looked like a bum as far as Hogue was concerned. Certainly he got no points for the quality of the company he kept.

"Why not hang out your own message," Hogue asked, "and leave me out of it?" It seemed a reasonable enough question.

"We'd kinda like things to be real normal around here until that train goes through," Chuck said. "And we'd like the message to be normal too. You know. The right form. The handwriting they're used to seeing outta this station. All that. It wouldn't hardly do to tip them that anything's different today. Wouldn't do at all." He crossed his legs and leaned back with his hands hooked around an upraised knee, a perfect picture of a relaxed human being in a state of idle contentment.

"Just to be sure about that," he went on, "we brought along our friend J. Kenneth Harlinton here." He smiled slightly at the incongruity of referring to such an obvious tramp by such a formal name. "J. Kenneth used to be a telegrapher for the Yew Ess Gov'ment. It's a fact. It's a fact. Back during the Big Wah, that was. Pronounced 'war' if you're a Yankee. Which J. Kenneth was. I wasn't, myself, but I don't hold it against him any more.

"Anyway, J. Kenneth is just gonna sit here and kinda listen to what comes in over that noisy contraption you got in the corner there, and he's gonna listen to anything you send *back* over that thing, an' if you try to tip anybody to what we're doing, well . . . you get the idea."

"If you don't," Al added, "you soon enough will." He stroked the scratched wooden grips of his revolver and looked like he would positively enjoy an excuse to use the thing.

There are sons of bitches, Hogue reflected, and there are sons of bitches. Among them, he thought, Al seemed to be a prince of sons of bitches.

"Like you said," Hogue muttered, "it's no skin off my nose."

"*That's* the right attitude," Chuck said encouragingly. "No fuss, no trouble and we go away soon. We won't be back to bother you again."

Hogue sighed. In a way they were right, actually. The railroad probably was well insured against thefts. Certainly

ought to be if it wasn't. And it was not like there was anything at stake here except a few dollars. Well, perhaps more
than a few dollars. Quite a few dollars or it would not be
worth all this effort to stage a robbery. That was logical.
There was a good bit of mining going on in the mountains
nowadays, and miners have to be paid. Without the mines
and the miners there would be no need for the railroads to
serve them, so without them Hogue would not be here to
begin with. And while Hogue might be willing to take his
pay on a company account kept in some dim office in Pueblo,
it was pretty well known anywhere in this part of the country
that miners are a contrary lot. Cowhands—which Hogue no
longer was, exactly, but whose attitudes he still carried—
thought of underground miners as slightly worse than daft at
their best and somewhere the far side of insane as a general
rule. Unlike normal people, i.e. cowhands, who would take
their pay in any hard coin including silver (although not in
any form of paper, which *everyone* found suspect), hard-rock
miners insisted on being paid in the same yellow metal they
were hauling out of the ground. They would take their pay
only in gold coin. And therefore the coins had to be hauled in
from somewhere else. The stuff was mined out here, but it
had to be refined and minted elsewhere, which meant mining
payrolls had to be transported into the mountains just as the
crudely smelted gold had to be hauled out of them.

The result of those assorted facts and prejudices was that
there were payrolls of closely guarded gold coins being
shipped into the high country from time to time. And this
crowd Hogue was now having to deal with, or to ignore as
best he could, seemed to think there was such a shipment on
the 1:20 westbound.

Hogue sat silently thinking what a dandy trick it would be on Chuck and Al and friends if there was nothing on that train but bolts of cloth and kegs of nails and such mundane articles of freight as that.

A dandy trick, he conceded, but hardly his problem.

His problem as he saw it was to get these bothersome people off his back just as quickly as possible with a bare minimum of trouble.

If that meant the train would be robbed, well, that was the MK&C's problem.

It really was not like they were asking him to cause any real damage. A few minutes of delay on some siding between here and the Pueblo terminus would cause no harm. There were no eastbound trains the westbound would run afoul of even if it was delayed an hour. So it was not like they were telling him to cause a wreck.

And a mild concern about the likelihood of a head-on collision was about as far as Hogue Bynell was willing to become interested in this nonsense between the railroad and a pack of would-be train robbers.

After all, it was not as though Hogue himself was some sort of railroader who actually cared about the railroad line. He performed as was expected from his end of things, and they did the same from theirs. There was no affection involved on either side. It was expected of him that he would not allow any collisions to take place. But no one had said anything about him having to take any guff off a bunch of armed robbers.

So it really was not his worry, he reasoned.

He would write their fake train order and they would ride away and that would be the end of that. In the meantime all

CHAPTER 7

Chuck and Al were sitting side by side on a pair of kegs muttering to each other, and J. Kenneth Whateverhisnamewas was sitting beside them but somehow managing to keep himself apart from them, among them but not really *with* them. A different breed of carp altogether, Hogue thought.

Not that he cared. About any of them. He reminded himself of that sternly, several times, and believed it. An obvious rummy like J. Kenneth Whozits—he could not remember the last name—was of no possible interest to him. The fact that J. Kenneth was a former telegrapher gave them no more of a meeting ground than if the man had once been a circus acrobat. Hogue Bynell was employed as a telegrapher for the sake of expedience, pure and simple. If he could no longer work as a cowhand it did not necessarily follow that he no longer was, or would have preferred to be, a cowhand. That he was and expected to remain. The railroad and the clattering wires meant nothing to him. Nothing at all.

He closed his eyes and tried to shut out the presence of the other three men.

They would wait here for a short time. They would do what they had come to do. And they would leave. Now or later, they were of no real interest to him.

Deliberately Hogue let his thoughts wander. That was a

dangerous thing at times and something he usually tried to avoid, but now he welcomed the distraction.

Once, back when he had been a whole man, he had been considered—had been, actually—a lusty man, whether with beef or bottle or bed. Those times were past now, submerged in the embarrassment and the shame he felt when he was among strangers, but there were times when he could not help but remember the way things had been.

Now he welcomed the reverie of some of those times, deliberately dwelling on thoughts he might otherwise have avoided, thinking about the times when he and Goodnight and Jimmy and others in the brawling Y Knot crew would head for town and for the blowouts that invariably accompanied any break from the dull, difficult routine of ranch work.

He remembered this fight and that saloon and some bawd and before long his forehead showed a slick sheen of new sweat, and Hogue knew that if he did not force his thoughts away from such things in very short order he would very soon have to request some time away from the relay station and make another unwelcome trip into Pueblo just to satisfy the demands that a man's body will impose on him no matter how much he may despise the weaknesses of his own flesh.

Hogue wiped the back of his forearm across his head and, without thinking, for the moment almost entirely forgetting the presence of the others, reached into his bottom desk drawer for the bottle he always kept there.

The bottle was uncorked and raised halfway to his lips when he realized his mistake and paused with the container poised in midair while he glanced quickly toward the would-be robbers.

If he had hoped the object in his hand would not be noticed, he was disappointed. All three of his unwelcome guests had stopped whatever they might have been doing a moment before and now sat looking at him and at the bottle of cheap whiskey. Hogue cussed himself rather thoroughly as he saw Al's eyes widen and the dawning spread of a smile on the lean, bearded face of the fellow. It was too late entirely to shove the bottle back into the drawer and pretend that it did not exist.

Still, he tried. He jammed the cork back into the slender neck of the bottle and without haste replaced the jug in the drawer. Maybe—

"Don't be so quick to hide that purty thing," Al said with a grin. "It wouldn't be friendly of you t' not offer a man a drink"—Al gave him a smile that contained all the charm and friendliness not of the Hindu flutist but of the snake the flutist might be trying to impress—"crip," he added.

Hogue gave Al a stony stare in return. Al had not found a virgin when it came to name calling; Hogue had been called a cripple before. And a great deal worse.

"I'm not your friend," Hogue said softly, "and so far you haven't given me all that much reason to think of you as a man." The desk drawer remained closed.

Al began to chuckle. He stood and dropped a half-smoked cigarette onto the plank floor, stepping over the butt and allowing it to smolder where it was while he glided with a probably deliberate show of casual grace across the floor to Hogue's desk.

"I really do think," Al said, "that you oughta change your mind and try to be sociable here."

Hogue swiveled his chair to face the door and tried to ignore the lanky gunman who was standing over him. His anger— he had to keep swallowing it back, had to keep reminding himself that Hogue Bynell no longer had the right to anger and defiance and pride. Whole men might have that right. Hogue Bynell did not. It was a difficult thing to remember at times. A taste of bile rose in his throat, but he swallowed that back too. He tried to ignore the man and at the same time to not seem to be cringing from him. He might have managed either of those separately, but the combination was proving difficult to handle.

Al laughed. He did not sound particularly upset. "Oh well," he said, "if you won't offer, I reckon we'll have to help ourselves."

Al placed a steadying hand on Hogue's right shoulder and leaned heavily onto the one-legged man as he bent over and pulled the desk drawer open. He got the bottle and put all of his weight onto Hogue's shoulder as he straightened up into a standing position again. "Thanks. I really didn't think you'd mind." He laughed again and carried the bottle back to the keg, where he took a long drink himself before offering the bottle to the others. Neither Chuck nor J. Kenneth joined him.

Hogue had some fleeting thoughts about kicking himself, then thought bitterly that that was a hell of a poor idea for a one-legged man. Use his lone leg to kick himself with and he would fall flat on his face. Or in the other direction. For a brief moment he idly wondered just which way a one-legged man *would* fall if he tried to kick himself where he needed it the most.

Chuck, in the meantime, seemed to have acquired a look of vague distaste. Or perhaps it was unease. He glanced sideways toward his partner, who was now taking his third or fourth long pull at the bottle. The container had been a quarter full; now there was little left. Al was knocking it back more heavily than a sensible man normally would.

"Join me," Al said in a too-loud voice. But he did not offer the bottle to his partners again.

Within a few minutes the jug was empty. Al tossed the dead soldier into the open door of the potbelly stove with a clatter of breaking glass, and Hogue began to cuss some more. He would have to clean the stove out before he could light it the first time he wanted to use it this year. The labor was no less than he deserved, he quickly decided. He should have known better than to show a whiskey bottle to a robber.

Al leaned back and rubbed his fingertips up and down his belly. He belched once and grinned. "Lousy stuff," he declared, "but it sure beats creek water."

Chuck grunted something in return. J. Kenneth was ignoring both of them.

They were not, Hogue decided, a particularly close or brotherly crew of train robbers.

"You know," Al speculated, "I'll just bet you that where there's one thing of interest, say a jug or a gun or even a pile of cash money, why, there might be something else that ain't been shared and maybe oughtn't to be overlooked." He grinned. "Just to make sure we all stay friends here while we're waiting. You know." He got up again and began to prowl around the tiny interior of the relay shack.

CHAPTER 8

Hogue stared stonily forward, toward the doorway and the blank side wall of the shack. Behind him he could hear Al rummaging untidily through the few things that Hogue owned. If things had been different. . . . Hogue shook his head. Things were not different. He was what he was, as little as that happened to be now, and he could not change it. He just had to wait it out. They would be gone soon enough, and—

The back of his head exploded into a sheet of unexpected pain, and Hogue's upper body jammed suddenly forward into the hard edge of the desk.

"You were holding out on me. Sonuvabitchin' cripple, you were holding out on me." There was more triumph than anger in Al's voice.

Hogue knew what he would see, but he turned to look anyway. Al had found the bottles—four of them there were —in the wooden crate Hogue kept under his bed.

"If I'd tried to hide them I would have done a lot better job than that," Hogue said mildly. His head hurt and there was an ache of pain remaining in his chest, but he tried to let neither show. He wondered what Al had hit him with. Surely not with a fist. Still, he did not feel any blood running down the back of his neck. And he would not give the outlaw the satisfaction of seeing Hogue reach back there in search of blood.

Al was laughing again, a higher-pitched sound than before. The laughter did not sound altogether rational to Hogue. The man seemed awfully pleased with his discovery.

Al uncorked one of the fresh bottles, took a long pull at the opening and renewed his search among Hogue's personal belongings. Hogue turned away. He did not particularly want to watch the performance, and there was nothing he could do to stop it.

"I think you made a bad mistake," Chuck observed. He was speaking to Hogue, but his eyes were on Al.

"He's your partner," Hogue said, half accusing and half hopeful.

"My partner, your problem," Chuck agreed.

J. Kenneth was still ignoring all of them.

Chuck began to roll a cigarette. He and Al both smoked entirely too much, as far as Hogue was concerned. He cared only because of what the two of them were managing to do to his floor. The place might be a dump, but it did not have to be a pigsty as well. And after all, Hogue had to live in it, while they would be able to walk away anytime they wished, on two sound legs apiece.

Hogue tried to build a good hatred for them, for all three of them, but he had barely begun when the telegraph receiver opened with a clatter that must have sounded like just so much aberrant noise to the uninitiated. To Hogue it was the call sign opening his key and identifying the incoming message as being for Relay 12.

By habit, Chuck and Al and their intrusion were forgotten, and his attention was on the rattle of the electromagnetic receiver, his hand already reaching for a fresh pencil and an always present message pad.

He began to write, his fingers quickly catching up with the letters that had already been sent and then smoothly following the flow of sound, translating clicks and clacks into written letters that formed words he did not bother to read while the message was being sent. It was entirely possible for a good operator to take down messages flawlessly by the hour without ever once himself reading what he was writing on his pad. Hogue's instructor had been able to take down incoming copy without an error while maintaining a perfectly normal conversation completely apart from anything contained in the messages. And the instructor claimed to know a man—Hogue had never met him and was not sure if he believed it—who could take down a message with one hand and send another, quite separate message with the other hand. Hogue had been totally skeptical about that when he was still learning how to read the noisy wire; now he was not so sure, although he still did have some doubts.

When the message was complete, Hogue automatically threw the brass switch to turn his sending key on and tapped out a quick receipt for the message.

It was routine stuff, Hogue saw when he read it. A pickup order for two empty cattle cars that had been on a siding east of Relay 12. There was probably a great urgency involved, Hogue thought dryly. The cars had been on the siding for two and a half months to his own certain knowledge. The order was to be put on the hook for the regular afternoon eastbound, which would come through sometime after Chuck,

Al and company had finished their business here and gone away. Hogue would not mind posting it then. Far from it.

He shoved the pad aside. He could transpose the message onto the proper form and bag it later and—

He stopped in the midst of his line of thought.

They had *told* him that J. Kenneth Whatshisface was an old army telegrapher. But for damn sure nobody had *shown* him that.

Interesting. And after that unnecessary whack on the head, it would not hurt Hogue's feelings even a little bit if he could get away with a message to alert Pueblo and Relay 10 about what was coming.

He folded the slip of paper he had just copied the newly arrived message onto and stuck it into his shirt pocket.

"In case you're wondering," he said to no one in particular, "that was routine traffic. The westbound will be twelve minutes behind the normal schedule. Loose ballast on the road between here and Relay 10, so they're ordered to reduce speed until a work crew gets it fixed."

Chuck nodded his acceptance of Hogue's lie, but J. Kenneth looked at him for the first time in quite a while and cocked his head.

After a moment the wizened little rummy smiled. His teeth and gums looked as though it had been a long time since he had taken any care of them.

"You are entitled, I believe, to the inquiry," he said, "but I must disappoint you." To Chuck he said, "Not that it matters, Charles, but the gentleman received an order for an eastbound engine to pick up several cars from a siding which they identify by a milepost location. I suspect you do not truly care where it is."

The man's voice—Hogue had not really noticed until then how completely quiet J. Kenneth had been—was totally unlike his appearance. Startlingly unlike it. Although he looked like a tramp off the rods, J. Kenneth sounded like a gentleman of some considerable culture and breeding. His voice was low on the tonal scale and very smooth. It sounded quite strange coming from such an unattractive source and no doubt was the reason for the formal references by initial and middle name. With the education and background the man must certainly have, Hogue thought, the reference was a biting and unkind reminder of some sort and certainly was no pleasantry to the man on the receiving end of such a crude form of humor. Hogue wondered briefly how J. Kenneth Whatsit had come to be tied up with a crew like Chuck and, particularly, Al. He decided almost as quickly that either J. Kenneth was one of those who believed that enough money would cure any ill . . . or the man had reached a point where he believed that nothing at all mattered anyway. If he had to take a guess, Hogue would judge it to be the latter.

Not that he cared.

Nor did Chuck seem to particularly care that Hogue had been lying to him. He shrugged once and looked away. Obviously he cared nothing about the railroad's affairs involving any trains other than the one carrying the payroll shipment. Hogue seriously doubted that the man would be so unconcerned if there were any development about that movement, though.

Hogue looked at J. Kenneth and shrugged. He got a tentative smile back in return.

But that answered that. J. Kenneth could read his wire exactly as advertised. So much for any thoughts of mutiny. Hogue yawned.

"What was that again, Mr. High-an'-mighty?" Al asked from behind Hogue's back. Hogue had almost forgotten the man, or more accurately had almost been able to force Al from his thoughts.

Patiently and politely, J. Kenneth repeated what he had told Chuck. Again Hogue was struck by the cultured tone of the man's voice.

"And this one-legged bag of manure lied to you about it, eh?" Al said with a giggle. Hogue wondered how much was left of that newly opened bottle Al had found a few minutes before. Too little, Hogue suspected. He chose to ignore the insult and concentrate instead on the state of the mind that had delivered it.

Al giggled again, and Hogue felt himself involuntarily stiffen. There was something about Al—

The back of his head exploded with pain for the second time, but at least this time he had a hand braced between himself and the cutting front edge of the desk. It was not quite as bad that way. At least the pain was contained in a single place this time.

"Mister," Hogue said calmly, "I been busted up by the meanest horses you ever seen an' prodded by the rankest bovines that ever walked out of Texas. If you think you're gonna make me break down an' bawl from a little ol' thump on the head, you're in for a disappointment, and that's a fact."

Al broke into a fit of loud, rasping laughter. "You sit there and talk mighty feisty, crip, but I don't see you tryin' to do nothing about it." He took a painful hold on Hogue's shoulder and spun his chair around so they were face to face.

"Yeah, you talk pretty feisty, but I don't think you got a white man's guts, crip. If you do, why, come ahead an' try me. I'll hop on one leg and everything. Just to make it square."

Al leaned close and breathed into Hogue's nostrils, glaring at him from scant inches away.

They stayed like that for some time. It seemed like minutes but must only have been seconds on a clock. Still, it was long enough to be uncomfortable. Hogue knew without looking that the other two were watching them, wondering themselves if the one-legged telegrapher would have the guts to accept the challenge and fight the half-drunk outlaw.

Hogue swallowed, hard. He wanted to. He wanted to haul off and bury his right hand wrist-deep in Al's belly. He wanted to, and from where he was sitting he was perfectly positioned to do just that. A few years ago he would have done that and a great deal more.

But that was years ago. And it was now that he had to make his decision: take his licking like a man or back off like a coward.

Hogue blinked. He felt empty inside. And . . . frightened. That was the truth. He had participated in half a hundred barroom brawls with and without friends to side him, and he had never once backed down from any man during all those years with the cow camps.

But that was then.

He blinked again and squinted his eyes shut. When he opened them again he shifted his gaze away from Al's accusing stare down toward the man's open collar. He willed his muscles to go slack, and he waited meekly for whatever Al might choose to do next.

Al laughed again, the outburst sending a fine spray of spittle into Hogue's face. Hogue turned his head away.

Al straightened and stood for a moment over Hogue. Finally he reached out and, lightly, with an insulting gentleness, patted Hogue on the cheek. Al turned to the others and said, "Don't worry none about this ol' cripple. He won't be bothering nobody again. An' *that's* the fact here."

CHAPTER 9

There had been a time. . . .

Hogue remembered one in particular, remembered it well. He had been working on a trail crew for John Blocker, moving a herd from the hill country north of San Antonio on their way to Ellsworth, where the buyers would be waiting with eager pens, ready to scratch off bank drafts in numbers much larger than Hogue or any of the other boys could hope to comprehend.

The herd had been carrying a Z1 road brand slapped on top of a dozen other ranch brands from all the places where the steers had been picked up. Not a very big herd, a little over two thousand head, which was not much by the standards of the time, but the steers had been acting like a bunch of mixed stock instead of like steers. They were spooky and rank and hard to handle. It wore the boys to a nubbin trying to keep them together, and they never did settle enough to begin putting on weight along the trail the way a well-managed herd should do. That was not Blocker's fault; Hogue had worked for the man before and knew that he was a better drover than that. It was just the way things had been working out.

The weather was against them, for one thing. Wet and unusually cold for the time of year. The crew could not sleep well and were tired all the time and argued with one another constantly. They were on edge and that probably contributed to the edginess of the bovines, and altogether it was turning out to be a bad drive. If Blocker had not had a rule about guns and sheath knives being kept locked up in a chest on the bed wagon, there might have been even more trouble than there was, Hogue realized.

Like nearly every other trail boss, Blocker also had a rule that there would be no liquor in camp, but the man was sensible. He was able to see that his crew was close to the point of breaking by the time they were into the Indian Nations, and he was bright enough to try to do something about it.

Hogue chuckled now and then when he thought about the Nations and how far from the truth lay all the popular conceptions of that country.

The penny dreadfuls—and the drovers read them as avidly as did any uninformed Easterner—painted the Nations as a place where a white man's scalp was always in danger. That was a crock of Grade A crap. In all the parts of it Hogue had seen, in all the parts he ever did see, it was a place where civilized Indians and rather uncivil whites ran stores and farms and businesses and where the blanket variety of red men begged and burnt lice and did whatever it was they did to keep themselves from starving. Which as far as Hogue could ever see had not been much.

Liquor was supposed to be outlawed by federal order all through the Nations, but no one has yet figured out a way to keep a man from making a fool of himself when he really wants to, and that was as true in the Nations as it was in Kansas City or Boston or any other place. The only difference was that in Kansas City they called the places saloons and in Boston called them bars and in the Nations called them hog

ranches. The quality of their wares might differ one place
from another, but the end result was always the same.

Anyway, Hogue remembered, they were passing within a
few miles of one of these hog ranches that sat on the bank of
a sometimes creek that now was running full due to all the
rain they had been having.

John Blocker stopped the herd on a flat of grass that was
better than it had any right to be except for that unusual
wetness and told the crew they would be able to spend a couple evenings relaxing in the hog wallow, taking turnabout
holding the herd while the others partied it up. That struck
everybody as a right fine idea.

Hogue was one of five boys who rode what was by then a
rather well-defined trail from the camp to the hog ranch for
the last trip there. Everyone else had had his time to relax,
and the herd would be heading north again in the morning,
and that probably had something to do with the attitude of
the people who hung around the place. Once this bunch was
gone there would be no further opportunity for any of them
to benefit from the cash Blocker had advanced to his men for
their evenings off.

The place had been no worse than Hogue expected, which
meant that it was pretty bad but did offer the several com-
modities the riled-up drovers had come in search of. The
whiskey was vile and the two available women were bone-
deep ugly, but, again, that was no worse than was expected.
They were there, which was all the cowhands asked.

The corners of Hogue's mouth twitched and he came very
close to smiling when he remembered the boys he had been
with that night.

Billy Barbero was a kid making his first trail drive, and he had passed out early in the festivities, which probably saved him, at least temporarily, from getting a dose of the social disease that inflicted nearly every trail hand.

Tom Crowley got sick to his stomach a little while later and made the place smell even worse than it had to begin with, which Hogue would not have thought possible if he had not experienced it himself. Tom volunteered to take Billy back to camp with him, which left three from Blocker's crew in the place.

Mort Oliver found a place to curl up in a corner of the dirt floor next, and Bug-Eyed John Sneffels keeled over a little time later. They had seemed to be having a good time; Hogue still was. He laughed at them and called for another drink.

The next time Hogue looked around, some greaseball of a buffalo hunter who probably had not been sober enough to shoot a rifle accurately in the past several years was busily trying to enrich himself by going through the pockets of Hogue's fallen friends. A dumpy squaw with just as much grease in her hair, whom Hogue knew from recently past experience was not half as lively as a man would like, was acting as the buffalo hunter's assistant in that operation.

They probably thought Hogue was too far gone to notice or to care if he did happen to notice, but Hogue Bynell had never been high on the notion of letting a friend down.

Hogue knocked back what was left in his tin cup—after the first few you could not taste it anyway, which was a blessing—let out a croak that was intended to be a lion's roar and began a stumble-footed charge at the offending pair.

Hogue felt himself grinning now toward the unseen doorway of the forgotten railroad shack.

That had been a fight to remember.

He was more than a bit foggy between the ears to begin
with. He reached them and launched a powerful right toward the buffalo hunter's jaw, but the punch somehow went
astray and connected instead with the squat, brown woman.
Which might have turned out to be a blessing, considering
all the tales Hogue had heard about what a squaw can do to a
man. Anyway, she was out of it as completely as the other
Blocker men were, right then and there.

Hogue lost his balance and fell plumb on top of the
buffalo hunter and Bug-Eyed John, which did not seem to
bother Bugs any but did knock the wind out of the buffalo
hunter. Both he and Hogue came to their feet weaving and
puny after that.

The hunter, who was very nearly as drunk as Hogue was,
made the mistake of trying to work on Hogue's midsection.
The theory was all right there, but the application left something to be desired. Hogue's belly was about as hard as it was
broad, and all that windmill flailing was taking as much out
of the buffalo hunter as it was out of Hogue.

In the meantime Hogue was taking some wild swings of
his own, aiming them in the general direction of the buffalo
hunter's head and letting fly. The fourth or fifth massive
punch connected by some fluke of fortune, and the buffalo
hunter went out like a candle in a windstorm.

Hogue stood over the assortment of fallen bodies and wondered if he should join them or if it would be worth the effort
to stay on his feet.

The buffalo hunter turned out to have some friends in the
place, though, and before Hogue knew what was going on a

couple of them had him wrapped up from behind and were turning him around to where they could do some damage.

There were three of them, all more or less drunk but certainly carrying less of a load than Hogue was, and two of them were engaged in the task of pinning Hogue's arms to his sides from behind him. The third planted himself at Hogue's front and let fly.

With the assistance of his two friends, the man landed a beauty, flush on Hogue's jaw. It should have dropped him like a barrow in a slaughterhouse, and no doubt the three thought the fight was over and they could begin picking pockets where their buddy had left off.

Instead, for some reason the impact served to clear Hogue's head of the blurriness the alcohol had brought on. He shook his head and stuck out his jaw and spat out some of the blood that was beginning to collect in his mouth from the impact. He grinned at the man who was standing in front of him, and the fellow's eyes widened.

"All *right*," Hogue told him.

A flexing of massive shoulder muscles and a powerful surge upward with his arms shook off the two who were clinging to him from behind.

It was still three to one, but now it was a great deal more equal than Hogue's opponents had intended.

The one who had been doing the punching tried to take care of it with a boot to the crotch, but Hogue blocked that with his thigh and, willing to accept a good idea when he saw one, planted the pointed toe of his own boot square on the offender's jewels. The man doubled over with a high-pitched squeal and was not heard from again.

"Two to go," Hogue said cheerfully as he turned to face the pair behind him.

They came at him in a rush of flying fists, seemingly so many and so busy that it looked to Hogue like it should have required twice as many men to throw so many punches.

He did not even try to sort out what belonged to whom but ignored the flurry about his ears and stomach, accepting the punishment they gave, aware of it without being particularly concerned about it. He could feel the dull thump of their fists but did not find the repeated impacts to be especially painful.

He laughed out loud and chose the one on his left as a primary target, concentrating on that one and ignoring the other.

A hard left over the heart brought the man's hands down, and Hogue formed his right hand not into a fist but into a knuckle-forward wedge that had the approximate consistency of a sash weight. This he stabbed with considerable force under the man's chin to a point immediately above the Adam's apple.

Which left only one for him to deal with.

That lone gentleman no longer seemed inclined to continue the contest. He looked at his fallen companions and turned very nearly as bug-eyed as Bug-Eyed John Sneffels. Immediately thereafter he turned and tried to run.

"Whoa up there, neighbor," Hogue said happily.

He grabbed the fellow by the nape of his neck and without thinking about the strength that was required picked him bodily off the dirt floor. The man screamed.

There probably was no need for further combat, but Hogue was not thinking about that at the time. He set the man back onto his feet, turned him around, took careful aim at the unresisting figure and laid the man out with a solid right cross that landed flush on the side of the fellow's unprotected jaw.

Hogue stood towering over the now numerous bodies that littered the floor of the filthy hog ranch, feeling strong and pleased and quite content to get back to work chasing those miserable bovines come morning.

He stood over them. . . .

He *stood*. That was the key to the whole thing.

A wave of bitterness swept through Hogue, wiping out the remembered sense of pleasure as if it had never been.

That had been from another time. It might well have been another man.

At least then Hogue had been a man. Now. . . .

He sighed. If he was going to spend the rest of his days hobbling around with one leg beneath his belt—and he damned sure was going to do that—it would be so much easier if he could forget that he had ever had two good legs to hold him upright, the way a man should be.

Someone born with only one leg would have much less of an idea about what he was missing. Hogue's memories would not allow him that slim measure of relief from torment. And the game of "if only" held no relief at all.

Hogue cursed softly to himself and cocked his head. Behind him he could hear Al alternately taking a gurgling swallow from Hogue's bottle and rummaging noisily through Hogue's personal belongings.

And there was not a thing a one-legged man could do to stop him.

Hogue wished that bottle was in his hand instead of Al's. At least *that* he still could do.

CHAPTER 10

"Well, well, what *do* we have here?" Al had given up searching through Hogue's private things around his bunk and was rummaging now through the desk drawers immediately beside the relay operator. It was becoming more and more difficult for Hogue to ignore him.

Al straightened and grinned and held up a small metal box that was held closed by a hasp but had no lock. There had never before been any reason to put a lock on anything in the shack. Hogue would not have thought about such a precaution.

Now Hogue was regretting that. He grunted softly to himself as he turned his head away and willed himself not to look at the grinning Al while the man pawed the box open.

"Now, what kinda goodies do we have here?" Al asked no one in particular. "A little stash of—" He cursed and pulled a handful of now crumpled paper from the box. "No money at all, crip? Nothing but this junk?" He cussed some more. Al sounded disappointed and annoyed at the same time.

With any luck, Hogue thought, the creep would throw the letters away. Burn them if he wished. Hogue should have burned them himself long since and now wished that he had done so. He did not know why he saved them anyway. They were the letters Mabel Cutcheon had sent him. He had no reason to save them.

But he did not want some miserable stranger pawing through them, regardless.

Hogue thought about turning, snatching the wad of papers from Al and tossing it into the stove, setting the letters afire. He thought about it, but he did not make any motion to do it. Instead he kept his eyes averted.

"Bunch o' crap," Al grumbled. He took another drink from Hogue's bottle.

"Is there anything there that we should be interested in?" Chuck asked. "They must be important if they were put away like that."

"It don't look like it."

Hogue could hear Al sorting through the letters. Then the man was still. Reading, Hogue thought. If the bastard could read. There were enough who could not.

Apparently Al was not among the ranks of the unwashed illiterates. Unwashed, yes, but not illiterate. After a few moments he began to chuckle.

"Hey, I ain't believing this," Al said. "This ol' crip has himself a lady friend. Serious. I ain't lying to you." No one challenged the statement, but Al went on as if someone had. "Listen to this, will ya: 'My *dear* Mister Bynell.' That's the way . . . just a minute. . . ." There was the soft rustle of paper before Al said, "Mabel. That's the way she signs it. Not Miss something nor Missus something, but ol' Mabel. Just her first name."

Al reached up and poked Hogue painfully below the ribs. "Are you close to that, crip? You been gettin' some from ol' Mabel? Is that why she signs her name so loose, huh?"

Hogue felt the heat rise in his face, but he remained silent. He sat quiet and helpless, knowing there was nothing he could do about this or about any of the rest of it. He damn sure should have burned those letters a long time ago. It was his own fault that he had not.

"Let's see what the ol' hussy has to say in here," Al mumbled with obvious pleasure.

There was a minute or more of silence while Al read through the letter in his hand.

"Huh!" Al said with a snort after a time. "She says she's needin' you to come trim her wicks again." The man laughed nastily. "Nothin' about dippin' your wick but some about you trimming hers. You a regular visitor there, crip? Or just when she can't find nothing better to warm her up? I'll bet that's it. A one-legged man, there's gotta be lots better around. I'll bet you just get the crumbs when she can't find nothing else. An' at that she must be a greasy ol' hawg to give you any time in there atall. Ain't that the truth, crip? Well, ain't it?" He poked Hogue in the ribs again. Hogue ignored the pain. Tried to ignore both kinds of pain the man was causing.

"Well, answer me."

"You already know it all," Hogue said. "I can't tell you nothing."

Hogue kept his eyes away from Al. In doing so he caught a brief flicker of expression on J. Kenneth Whatshisname's gaunt, pinched face. It might have been sympathy. It might as easily have been disgust. Hogue was not sure. Not that it mattered. All three of them would be gone soon. Whenever that was it would not be soon enough.

He looked at Chuck, too. The stocky outlaw seemed content enough for the moment. Perhaps because Al had been diverted by the letters and was no longer so diligently sucking at the whiskey bottle. Probably Chuck cared nothing about what else went on inside the shack as long as it did not interfere with the robbery they planned.

With a sharp bark of laughter Al went back to his letter reading, and Chuck began to roll another cigarette. J. Kenneth looked as though he was uninterested in the whole thing.

Hogue tried to assume the same sense of detachment that J. Kenneth was exhibiting. Hogue had had enough practice in the last year or so at the art of shutting the world out. It should have been easy for him by now. Somehow this time it was not quite as simple as it should have been.

CHAPTER 11

It was not like that at all. Al Trapp's snide suggestiveness could not change a single grain of the real truth, and the real truth was that Mabel Cutcheon was a good woman.

A far better woman, in fact, than Hogue Bynell deserved. He had believed that much *before* the accident. He felt it to be all the more true now.

A hussy, Al had called her, with his dirty mouth and obscene thoughts. Well, Hogue was no halo-bearing saint himself. Often enough he had joined the other boys in wisecrackery and dirty jokes. But he never would have applied any of them to a woman like Mrs. Cutcheon. No one who saw her could ever do that.

Mabel Cutcheon was anything but a trollop, as anyone could plainly see with a single glance.

That kind wore feathers and face paint as if to advertise themselves as being no better than a squaw.

Mrs. Cutcheon wore no makeup at all save an occasional dusting of powder, as was proper for a lady, and her hair was always, at least in public, kept neatly pinned into a bun. Her eyebrows were properly unplucked and her limbs always decorously covered. Hogue doubted that the freckled skin of that vee beneath her throat, where a man's flesh will become wrinkled and leather-hued from exposure by an open collar, had ever seen the light of the sun.

Not that Mabel Cutcheon was prudish. She was not; certainly not in the privacy of her own rooms.

She was a warm and giving person, cheerful and honest and fully human.

She was a lady, plain and simple, and the likes of Al Trapp had no business dragging a good woman's name down to their own crude level.

Hogue fought back a pang of resentment. He was no longer man enough to leap to the lady's defense. He had to keep reminding himself of that.

With a sigh half of impatience and half of annoyance, he forced such thoughts from his mind and tried instead to think of other, better things.

For instance, the time that particular letter referred to. Hogue remembered that well. Better than he really wanted to. He tried nowadays to keep such memories out of mind, for they were not always easy to bear.

That time had been, he thought—no, he was quite sure, actually—the first time he had visited Mrs. Cutcheon's home following the accident. The first time he had gone there on crutches with a pants leg pinned up.

She had visited him, frequently, while he still lay in the doctor's clinic bed, and she had insisted on this outing to her home as soon as he learned to operate his crutches without help. Dinner at the Cutcheon house was to be his first trip away from the clinic—which the doctor liked to dignify by calling it a hospital—by himself.

The distance was nearly five blocks, but Hogue had managed it. At the time, he was still taking his weight on the tender sockets of his armpits and had not yet learned to use his hands and arms to accept the strain, so by the time he reached the familiar doorway he was uncomfortable and in need of rest.

Mabel had had sense enough to allow him to negotiate the front steps on his own, without offering him any assistance, although he had seen the stir of a frilly curtain at her front window and knew she was already aware of his arrival and would be there watching in case he should fall. He had been grateful to her for that measure of understanding, and he thought at first that the dinner would be accomplished with less embarrassment than he had been expecting, and dreading, might happen.

He knocked at the closed and curtained front door, and she had waited a decent interval before answering his knock.

She led him to the small parlor, where he had visited more than a few times in the past, before the accident, and if she moved perhaps a bit more slowly now than she had done before, allowing Hogue to keep pace with her, she at least did not make a show of it, and again Hogue was grateful to her.

They talked for a while, about inconsequential things like the state of business at the dry-goods store she was still operating after the death of her husband, like her difficulties in securing a good clerk to handle her business affairs and in finding reliable suppliers for the many things she needed to maintain in stock.

Hogue really had as little interest in the affairs of a dry-goods store as she probably did in the operation of a beef ranch, but the topics were comfortably neutral and the conversation was more important for its own sake than for its content.

She offered him a glass of wine, which he accepted, and drank one with him. She was, after all, not a prude and held no convictions that would condemn a drink or two for a man nor a sip or two for a lady.

After a decent interval she led him into the tiny niche that served her for a formal dining room, and he took a chair at the head of the table, where her husband had used to sit. That was, Hogue realized, the first time he had been invited to sit in that particular spot. Always before, he had been seated across from Mrs. Cutcheon at the side of the rectangular table. He wondered if the change might have some significance.

The table had already been laid with the best she had to offer. If not elegant by Boston standards, the table settings were certainly far finer than Hogue was used to dining from, either in a cow camp or at the clinic.

A pair of coal-oil lamps with hand-painted decorative shades gave scant but attractive light to the small room, and Mabel did not offer to light any more for their meal.

The food had been ready in advance of his arrival, waiting in her warming oven, and she served it with a minimum of fuss. They ate largely in silence, but Hogue found it to be a comfortable silence and the food to be exceptionally good. He did not think his judgment of the meal had been affected by its comparison with the plain fare he was accustomed to at the clinic, either. Mabel Cutcheon was quite a good cook, as was amply demonstrated by that dinner.

Later she left him in the parlor with a cigar and a glass of raspberry brandy for company while she "rid up" in the kitchen.

Hogue felt very nearly comfortable for the first time since he had awakened to the sight of that ugly, barren, flat expanse of sheet in the bed where his leg should have been.

While Mabel was busy in the kitchen, he tried to repay her kindness with a gesture of thanks.

Practically none of the lamps in the house seemed capable of producing a clear, steady butterfly of light. Why there seemed to be no woman born who could ever properly trim a lampwick Hogue did not know, but that seemed an axiom that no man could ever understand.

At any rate, he took out his pocketknife and whetted it carefully on the counter of his scuffed left boot and, crutching slowly from one table to the next, proceeded to trim and clean every wick in every lamp in the parlor and the vestibule. He was working on the lamps in the dining room when Mabel completed her chores in the kitchen and caught him at his work.

"That is exactly the task Mr. Cutcheon used to undertake. Every Sunday afternoon before nightfall, without fail," she told him. "You have no idea, Mr. Bynell, the things a woman comes to miss when there is no man in the house."

Hogue shrugged. "Is it Sunday?" He had lost track of the days and had no idea.

"No, but. . . ." She stopped there and looked slightly embarrassed. "You've come to know me well enough,"—she hesitated—"Hogue"—the use of his first name alone was quite rare—"that I should be able to tell you . . . I am past the point of missing Mr. Cutcheon now. But I have been missing the visits you used to pay here before. . . ." She repeated firmly, "Before." It was enough. He knew before what.

"Yes, ma'am." Now it was Hogue's turn to be embarrassed. He knew quite well what she was referring to now.

Mabel Cutcheon was a good woman but a human one. She

admitted, delicately, to needs and desires that Hogue had never known ladies had. Before Hogue's accident, she had shared with him moments that a crude type like Al Trapp could never understand and which, somehow, had done nothing to lessen her in Hogue's perception. She remained a good woman in Hogue's view.

Now, delicately, she seemed to be inviting him to continue the relationship they had begun, in spite of his disfigurement. Inviting him, he thought, to that and perhaps to something more.

His seating position at the table, the lighting during the meal, now her reference to the absence of a man in the house. He thought. . . . He had no right to such thoughts. Hogue had clamped down with bitter stubbornness on that. He had no right to think anything about this good woman.

Even so, Mabel Cutcheon had seemed to understand the difficulty he was having.

Abandoning her usually oblique forms of invitation and suggestion, she eventually became quite bold and—Hogue swallowed hard at the memory—offered herself to him as a woman gives to a man.

It had been—he squinted his eyes shut—a miserable experience. The worst of his life. Far worse than the accident itself. Perhaps worse even than that awakening to his new status as a castoff and a cripple.

For the first time in his life, Hogue Bynell had been unable to perform as a man.

And that had sealed him in his bitterness.

On that self-same visit when he had trimmed the wicks of Mabel Cutcheon's lamp and which Al, unknowing, had now made crude reference to.

Oh, there had been nothing in her letter, mailed long afterward, that would in any way refer to what had happened during that visit. There never would be.

Hogue remembered the letter quite well. That one and nearly all of the others. Always their tone was cheerful and circumspect and pleasant and warm and. . . .

And there was nothing that could ever come from them. Which was why Hogue had long since quit responding to any of those letters, which still continued to arrive with monthly regularity.

There was no point in his writing to her. Or to anyone. He was useless to any decent woman, and he knew it. And Al guessed it, more accurately than he would ever know.

Bastard, Hogue thought. If only. . . .

But "if only" gathers no cows. "If only" would not cause the clock to spin any quicker. Hogue was sick of "if only." All he wanted now was to be left alone. That would be quite enough. If only he could have that.

He shut his eyes and tried to shut out the sounds of Al pawing through Mabel Cutcheon's private letters to a man who no longer existed.

CHAPTER 12

There was never enough work at Relay 12 to keep even a one-legged man really busy, but at least the late morning usually gave Hogue something to do with himself. For no reason that he had ever bothered to wonder about, that period was usually when the line sent most of its wire traffic.

This day, the busy period started slightly earlier than usual. There was a special eastbound due at Relay 12 at 10:09. It would cause no interference with the westbound Chuck and Al and company were interested in, but Hogue was ordered to post for it a flimsy telling it to pick up the empty cars on the siding to the east and to rescind the previous train order originally intended for the regular P.M. eastbound.

Routine stuff, but now it irked him. It meant he would once again have to use his crutches in full view of his unwelcome guests.

Hogue looked at his watch: 9:53. My, he was thinking, how time flies when you are having fun. He scrawled the new train order onto a standard form ready for the pickup pouch, but even as he wrote the order and initialed it he was wondering if he should just let this one slide, post the order to the P.M. eastbound as he had first been told. The empties would arrive where they were needed regardless, and he would be saved that much more embarrassment. It would not be a victory over Al, by any stretch of the imagination, but. . . .

He glanced over at J. Kenneth, who was looking alert and interested in his surroundings for the first time in a considerable while.

No, Hogue decided, if he failed to post the order as he was instructed, J. Kenneth would tell the others about it, and then Hogue would have Al to deal with. Probably painfully. They would undoubtedly decide that he was trying to tip the line to a problem at Relay 12 by refusing his orders.

Bastards, he thought.

He rolled the flimsy into a cylinder and snapped a gum rubber band around it and dropped it into one of the pickup pouches that always lay beside his desk. He picked up his crutches and stood.

"Where are you goin' with that?" Chuck demanded. Hogue could feel, without looking, a threatening tension in Al behind him.

"It's a train order," Hogue snapped. "You want things to keep on going normally around here, don't you?"

Chuck looked pointedly at the former telegrapher, J. Kenneth.

The scrawny gentleman-turned-derelict nodded. "I read the order as he received it," J. Kenneth said. "Quite routine."

"You heard what that noise box said maybe," Chuck corrected him, "but you ain't seen what he put on that paper. Read it over. Make sure it's what it should be."

J. Kenneth shrugged. "Whatever you say." He did not wait for Hogue to crutch over to him with the pouch but instead came to Hogue. He unrolled the flimsy, read it, and replaced it in the pouch exactly the way it had been. "He attempted no surprises."

Chuck grunted.

"Can I get on with my work now?"

The stocky outlaw made an impatient gesture toward the platform, which Hogue took to be approval. Bastards, he thought again.

He made his way out onto the platform and stood for a moment looking toward the distant horizon, beyond the browning grass of the rolling plains toward the Picketwire and the flatter, drier country where a man had to fight heat and mesquite as well as cattle and boredom. A *man*, Hogue reminded himself bitterly. That was something he would not have to worry about ever again.

Still, standing outside there, where he could see the grass and the immensity of the sky and the big, beautiful emptiness that he had come to love, in spite of what remained inside the shack behind him he found himself breathing just a bit deeper and feeling just a bit fitter.

If only. . . .

Seven pronghorns were grazing idly on a knoll half a mile south of the station, and Hogue paused to watch them. For that brief period he did not feel bitter about any of it. He came close to smiling when one of the tiny figures, probably a calf (lamb? he did not know which an antelope should be called) bounded high into the air in a playful leap and raced around to the other side of the small herd.

Hogue thought briefly of the carving he had been working on before. He really would have to do another. Maybe even one good enough to keep. He had come to really enjoy the pronghorns in this past year or so. Always before he had thought of them as a source of meat. Now they were something closer to companions.

With a sigh, Hogue reminded himself that the eastbound special would be along in a few minutes. He crutched his way across the platform to the post where his pouches were hung and rigged the train order for pickup.

A wire loop carried the pouch on the hook, and the passing engineer could snag it with a short staff and hook of his own just by reaching out from his cab. There was no need for the trains to slow in their passage. It was an efficient system.

He had no particular desire to return to the company inside the shack, so Hogue leaned against the tall post and waited. Already he could hear the approach of the special from the west.

He looked up at the pouch dangling in the thin, healthful air of the high plains. Above it and mounted to the post was the red-ball flag that was also part of the standard railroad equipment. In all the time Hogue had been at Relay 12 he had never had occasion to flag a train, had never had a passenger come here to board a train. Still, it made no difference at all to the planners of the MK&C if a piece of equipment was going to be needed at any particular station. The standard-issue items were installed regardless, and anything that was not standard was absent unless an operator wanted to buy it out of his own pocket.

Hogue shook his head. The line was implacably set in its own ways, but at least it let him alone. There was that to be said for it.

He looked to his right. The special was closer now; he could hear it quite plainly. It seemed to be making good time.

For a moment, Hogue wondered what would happen if he tried to signal to the crew, tried to warn them somehow from—

He heard footsteps behind him and turned. Al was there, grinning. "Just so's you don't get any ideas," he said. "I'll be in the doorway there watchin' you. Move just a li'l bit wrong and I'll put a slug through your knee." He laughed. "I reckon you know which one."

Hogue turned his head away. Yes, he knew which one. There was only one.

Hogue thought about that for a moment and found himself trying to swallow against a suddenly desert-dry throat. It was bad enough as things were. The thought of losing his remaining leg too would be beyond his ability to bear. Absolutely beyond it, he knew.

That bastard Al had unerringly found the single greatest weakness Hogue Bynell could possibly have now, and Hogue had no doubts at all that the man would not be beyond using that weakness against him. On a whim as easily as by necessity. At least the others, Chuck and J. Kenneth, were interested in the outcome of a particular job. Al seemed to be just plain mean.

Hogue pretended to ignore the threat and turned to watch the rapid approach of the special.

The engineer spotted the hooked pouch waiting for him— there were trackside markers warning him well in advance of every station shack he would pass and alerting him to look ahead for possible orders—and Hogue could see the man lean out of his cab with a staff held casually in his left hand. This was something the engineer did several times daily.

Hogue did not know the man—he knew few enough of

their faces and practically none of their names, even on the work trains that stopped there once a week—but the striped cap and set of his chin were familiar enough. That was one thing about the engineers, Hogue admitted. There were no drunks or misfits or creeps among them. They were the elite of the line and, as far as they were concerned, the elite of all creation. They took their work seriously. Much more so than you would find with a half-wild bunch of crazy cowhands, at least half of whom would be looking for a practical joke to pull at any given moment.

The intensity of the engineers—and of a good many others on the line as well—had been hard for Hogue to accept at first. He was not entirely sure he had accepted it yet. Or that he cared enough to want to.

The railroaders were just damn-sure different from the boys he used to ride with.

Not as good, Hogue amended stubbornly. *Too* serious. A man ought to be able to have some fun in his work. Hogue sighed. He no longer expected to have any fun in anything.

The engineer deftly snatched the pouch with his hook and gave a short nod that might have been meant for Hogue or might have been simple satisfaction at making the pickup. By the time Hogue turned to look at the already receding engine, the engineer was back inside his cab and there was no sign of the pouch that had just been taken aboard.

Hogue stood braced on his crutches and his one good leg and felt the pull of the wind caused by the passage of the short freight a few feet from where he stood on the platform.

Having that much noisy, heavy steel and wood passing practically within inches had been rather frightening the first few times, but Hogue no longer thought about it.

He could hear the loping, protesting roll of the massive wheels over the rails and could smell the lingering scent of coal smoke when the train was gone, but in moments it was as if the special had never gone by.

There was a knoll just to the east of the station, and the tracks curved ever so slightly there, so the special was lost to view in very short order. Hogue did not miss it.

For the first time, though, he thought that perhaps he should have a bench put onto the platform so he could sit out here and watch the pronghorns at play. A bench would have come in particularly handy right now, as he did not really want to go back inside with Al and Chuck and J. Kenneth, but his only alternative would be to stand outside on the platform, where, too soon, his hands and armpits would begin to tire from the need to support himself on the crutches. Standing around on railroad platforms or street corners could no longer be considered a long suit.

He turned and began to make his way back to the relative comfort of his chair.

CHAPTER 13

The telegraph key had begun to clatter before Hogue was well into the shack, and he had to hurry the last few paces—swings, in his case—across the wooden floor. He swung hastily into his chair and let his crutches fall against the wall where the never-used flag lever was. More unnecessary but standard railroad equipment; Hogue had long since removed the bar-iron handle and used it now as a poker for his stove.

He had begun to receive the incoming message in his head before he ever reached his chair, and now his fingers flew as he caught up with the letters being formed one by one by the unseen telegrapher somewhere to the west.

Hogue accepted the message and receipted it from long habit, but this time when he threw the switch to disengage his key and sat back in his chair, he was wearing a deep frown instead of his accustomed scowl. He swiveled the chair to face the wall and sat there for some time in silence.

"You may as well tell them," J. Kenneth prompted after several minutes. "I did read it, you know." The man's tone of voice was not unkind.

Hogue grunted.

"So what was that all about?" Chuck demanded. Hogue turned the chair to face him, continuing to ignore Al. For the moment, though, Hogue did not speak.

"Well?"

"That message. . . ." Hogue's voice trailed off into silence again. He remained undecided what to do about it.

"I *know* that much, dammit. What'd it say? J. Kenneth?"

"Give the gentleman a moment to work it out in his own mind, if you please."

"Well I *don't* please. I'll do the workin' out around here. Now, what'd it say?"

J. Kenneth shrugged and waited for Hogue to speak.

"That was a message from Pueblo," Hogue said. "They're putting on a special this afternoon. Eastbound."

"It wasn't about the payroll train?" Chuck demanded quickly.

Hogue shook his head.

"So what, then? It don't mean anything to us."

J. Kenneth turned his head away and coughed softly into his closed fist.

"What it means," Hogue explained, as much to himself as to the robber, "is that there will be another train on the track this afternoon. Coming toward the one you want."

"So?"

"So I've been told if there's a delay of as much as fourteen minutes on that westbound payroll train, I'm supposed to notify Relay 16 to put the special onto a siding. Otherwise there might be an accident. A head-on, you see."

"There won't be no delay in the payroll train's schedule, will there?" Chuck asked suspiciously.

Hogue shook his head again. "I don't see much chance of it. The trainmaster's pure hell-on-wheels. They run it tight on this section."

"All right, then. We got no problems, right?"

"I didn't say that. Not exactly."

"What the gentleman is trying to get across to you," J. Kenneth injected, "is that a delay on the siding, such as we propose to create for our own, uh, particular purposes, such a delay would likely result in a head-on collision between the payroll train and the eastbound special. *That* is what he is trying to explain, Charles."

For a moment, Chuck looked worried. "Before the payroll train reaches the siding where the boys are waiting, you mean?"

J. Kenneth looked expectantly toward Hogue.

"No," Hogue said. "After it left there. Unless it took you less than fourteen minutes to rob the train, and I don't think that'd be real likely."

Chuck looked relieved. "If that's all, don't worry about it. Once we got the payroll, who cares what happens to the damn train."

Hogue turned his head away. Yeah. You bet. Who cares what happens to the damn train.

In a manner of speaking, Hogue did not either. It was only so much iron and wood. A train had no feelings. A train was not like a horse or a cow or even a pronghorn, that a man should care about it. A train did not feel or sweat or get tired. Not ever. It was just a thing. Or rather, a collection of things.

But there were *men* on that train. Those men were already somewhere to the east and right now were rolling this way. And somewhere to the west, probably making up in the Pueblo yard this minute, there were other men who would be riding the eastbound special later on in the afternoon.

Those men were not the cowhands Hogue used to ride with and who Hogue still cared about in spite of himself.

They were just a bunch of railroaders. Practically no better than foreigners, really.

But they were men, dammit. And they were depending on Hogue Bynell's abilities to keep them safe when they rode the steel rails.

Now here were these miserable sons of bitches telling Hogue Bynell to not worry about it. Go ahead and kill a bunch of railroaders. It wouldn't matter so long as the payroll was safely robbed before then.

Hogue shook his head and turned his chair once more to face the blank, undecorated wall of his tiny relay shack.

It was a stinking position he was in. That was all there was to it. Stinking. He wished that bastard Al had not finished off the bottle from the desk drawer. This was not a great day to stay sober. Hogue sighed and let his chin drop toward his chest while he glowered at the wall. The boards in front of him really should have been mirrors instead, because he felt like glowering at himself.

CHAPTER 14

Hogue was visualizing the siding. Avoiding thinking about the problems ahead, actually. He did not want to think about that.

He could practically see Chuck's and Al's gun-hung, bloody partners waiting there already.

Hogue knew the spot well enough. He and the other boys from the Y Knot had spent enough time there in the past, not waiting to commit a crime but just goofing off. It was a good spot for that. Or for hiding, which in essence was what the boys used to do there. Probably still did.

The siding looped to the north of the main line, a curving parenthesis of steel separated from the main track by only a matter of yards. For miles to east and west alike the land around it was flat, scarcely rolling grassland too sparsely covered to hide a fully grown jackrabbit.

Except for that outcropping just to the north of the siding tracks.

Hogue knew perfectly good and well why the gang of robbers had chosen that particular siding for their work. They chose it for the same reason that Hogue and the Y Knot crew used to go there.

Not seventy-five yards from the siding steel, there was one of those outcroppings of rock that show themselves here and there in the big-grass country. Sometimes red, sometimes gray but for some reason mostly yellow or almost white rock, the outcroppings are a little less usual than a clump of trees on the open grass but not much more so. Some places, they are actually quite common.

Hogue had no idea what caused them. There were those who said the rocks had once been buried and that the land had worn down around them. Others speculated that the land surface had been there first and some underground force had once caused the rocks to push up through the ground like so many jagged spears. Hogue did not know the truth about that. It could have been either way. Certainly most of the outcroppings were jagged enough to have come up after the land was formed. Some of them looked almost like giant spearheads. And all of them were weathered and pitted, some looking not unlike giant hunks of Swiss cheese with wind-gouged holes and pockets marring their flanks. Frequently where you found one formation you found a handful of them, covering several acres.

Once, up in Wyoming, where a bunch of them had gone with a small herd of heifers for delivery to an Englishman putting together a new ranching operation, Hogue had seen the place they called Hell's Half Acre.

That outcropping was like a cave without the roof on it. A pit containing a bunch of extremely jagged spires on its floor. Along the edges of the pit, beneath the drop-off from the flat ground above, they found enough buffalo skulls and bleaching bones to make a fertilizer collector a rich man in a single gather. Someone said the old-time Indians used to drive buffalo off the flat country to fall onto the spears of rock and die down below, back before the white men brought them rifles and ammunition to make that method of killing inefficient.

There were such places all through this country, and the one where the robbers were now waiting was a good one. For hiding in, anyway.

The outcropping covered perhaps a dozen acres, no more, and was clearly defined. The rock formations rose perhaps fifteen feet above the level of the land, and there were a bunch of the formations, each individual rock shaped something like the blade of a spade, and each one standing alone. There were patches of level, grassy ground between them, where a man could ride a horse and wind between the separate blades.

That was what had attracted the Y Knot boys there.

Frequently when they were working that section of the country they would slip into the rocks about noontime to take a bit of rest. Most times of the year you could find a little shade once you got in among the spears, and shade was a rare and valuable thing on the plains.

What was more, this particular outcropping was big enough that you could get all the way inside it. Most of them consisted of a few spires or lumps of rock, but you were on one side of the formation or the other. This one was massive enough that you could ride right inside it.

The attraction of that was that a foreman could ride right past or even circle plumb around it and never see a sign of any of his hands.

A fellow could slip in there and loosen his saddle, let his horse take some time to stand in the shade and blow, and the hand could stretch out on the ground and get a little much-

needed sleep before he headed out again to the heat and the
dust and the hard work of handling livestock.

Oh, Hogue had done it often enough. He and the other
boys. He could not count the noonings they had taken in
there. Or the number of afternoons they had lingered past
the nooning to talk and smoke and nap when they should
have been out earning their wages.

Hogue almost smiled at the memory. The feeling had been
very much like the ones he had had when he was a kid and
would slip away from the schoolhouse to hunt frogs or manu-
facture bark whistles or search for a piece of twine that he
could pretend was a real catch-rope and use to lasso stray
hounds. The feeling had been very much like playing
hookey, and the grown cowhands had enjoyed it quite as
much as schoolchildren always did.

Now there were a bunch of armed men hiding in those
rocks, waiting for Hogue to toll an unsuspecting train into
their trap.

The rocks were only a matter of yards away from the siding tracks, and a score of men could hide in them without
anyone from the train being the wiser.

If the train crew got a message—*when* the train crew got a
message—from Relay 12 ordering a layover, why, they would
lay over. There was no freight so valuable and no guard so
suspicious that a train order would be questioned, much less
disobeyed. Once Hogue hung that flimsy, the train would
stop on the siding, and that was that.

The robbers could come boiling out from the rocks and be
on them with guns drawn before the crew knew a thing
about what was coming. There would seem to be nothing

amiss that would give them any warning. The attack would come as a total surprise, which was undoubtedly what Chuck and his friends would want.

It should work to perfection, and the crew would not have a chance to defend themselves.

Which was perhaps just as well. Surrounded like that and with no warning, the crew and whatever guards might be on the train probably would not even try to defend themselves. There probably would be no time for it.

And the robbers would know that. They would have no reason to begin shooting. The whole thing should go off without anyone being hurt.

And that much Hogue could live with. Hell, the railroad carried insurance. Even if they did not, the line could afford the loss of one payroll. It was only money, after all.

But now. . . .

The way things were shaping up now, that robbery would go along just exactly the way it was supposed to. The gang would come out waving their guns, and the crew would see they had no chance, and the robbery would take place without anyone having to be hurt.'

But there was no way in hell even the most efficient bunch of train robbers could open a safe and unload a payroll of gold coins and take their leave within fourteen lousy minutes.

No way.

If they were smart—and Hogue had no reason to believe they were anything but; whoever had planned this had done a job of it—if they were smart they probably would take an extra moment to dump the steam pressure in the engine's boiler. That would give them that much longer to make a leisurely escape before the train could be brought back to a head of steam and roll on down to the next relay station to report the loss and get a posse moving out of Pueblo.

And that— Dammit, Hogue thought, that would mean the westbound freight would be somewhere on the track and again would be completely unsuspecting when the eastbound special came rolling toward them out of Pueblo.

Fourteen minutes of leeway, and that was all. Anything more and there was certain to be a head-on.

Hogue groaned aloud.

Sure you can see for a long way out on this flat country. But a railroad engineer does not have to drive his train the same way a teamster has to watch his draft animals. A train is going wherever the rails take it, and the engineer really does not have to pay much attention to what is ahead until the trackside markers tell him there is a station or a signal coming up.

There were not even herds of buffalo around any more for an engineer to have to worry about. A stray cow or two was the most interference an engineer could expect to find on his track, and those were not enough of a bother to be worth trying to stop for. Even if that could be done, which it probably could not; it takes miles of preplanning to bring a fast-moving freight to a full stop. Emergency halts were just not possible. The engineer had to shut down his driver wheels and signal to the brakemen to set their screws. The brakemen had to see the signal—they would not be looking for trouble, any more than the engineer would be—and clamber from car to car tightening wheels a few degrees at a time and then back to start all over again by retightening the first of the cars that were their responsibility.

So even if by some unlikely chance the engineers saw each

other in the distance, why, it would still be next to impossible for them to avoid a collision.

No, Hogue thought, if this robbery went ahead as planned, the odds were the next thing to pure certainty that there was going to be a collision.

And that men were going to die in the cabs of those two opposing engines running against each other on the same slim set of track.

And Hogue Bynell was going to be responsible for that. Because he was the man who would be passing the fake train order to the engineer aboard that westbound freight carrying the payroll.

That engineer, whoever he was, was very probably going to die as a result of Hogue's false order.

Hogue picked his chin up off his chest and set his jaw. He swiveled around to face Chuck Porter.

"I ain't gonna do it," he declared. "I ain't gonna send that train off to a certain head-on collision."

Al Trapp was still behind him, and Hogue felt like cringing in his chair. He tried very hard not to and to keep from showing the fear he was already beginning to feel clutching at his bowels.

"I just ain't gonna do it."

CHAPTER 15

Actually it did not hurt nearly as much as Hogue had antici-
pated.

The back of his head—that seemed to be a favorite spot for
Al to thump on—felt as though it had some cauliflower
lumps on it, and certainly the skin had parted here or there.
He could feel some blood trickling past his collar and down
his back.

But really it was not so bad.

For the most part he felt numb where Al had hit him. Tomorrow and for several tomorrows afterward it would hurt
much worse than it did now. Hogue knew that from frequent
experience in the past, both in fights and in the knocks a man
takes when he sets out to brand a calf or ear down a feisty
bronc. A kick in the jaw by the youngest and weakest of
calves is worse than the best punch a prize fighter might be
able to throw. And Hogue had absorbed his fair share of
kicks and gouges, one way or another.

So it really was not all that bad.

He shook his head to clear it. The wetness at the back of
his collar was more annoying than the pain.

"You're gonna change your mind, crip," Al said. He
sounded quite pleased about the whole thing.

"Nope. Can't do it," Hogue said stubbornly.

"Betcha you're wrong," Al said happily. He paused to take another long pull from the bottle he had been sucking on.

Hogue looked across the small room toward Chuck. The stocky robber was the only one around who might have any effect on Al Trapp's actions, and it was obvious from Chuck's bored expression that he really did not much care what Al might end up doing to the one-legged telegrapher.

J. Kenneth, well, Hogue thought, it did not matter a fig's worth what *he* thought about any of it. For what it was worth, which was nothing, the old rummy looked as though he was distressed by the thought of any physical violence. But both he and Hogue understood that he had no voice in the matter. This would be up to Al and possibly to Chuck if he bothered to take a position on it. Hogue suspected that Chuck might care about the results but not the methods.

"I think," Al said thoughtfully, "I just might start in to bustin' his fingers." The man grinned sloppily. He was beginning to look well on his way toward being drunk. "That's the way he makes his livin'. I reckon that might go a ways toward convincin' him of the error of his ways."

Chuck shrugged. He pulled the makings from his pocket and began to build a smoke.

"I would not if I were you," J. Kenneth said. He said it slowly, as if he were unwilling to enter the discussion.

Chuck looked at him with an expression of mild annoyance, but Al's rapidly darkened features made it look as though he would be as willing to devote his attentions to J. Kenneth as to Hogue.

"We di'nt ask you about it," Al snapped.

"I was merely going to mention," J. Kenneth said, "that

our plan here is for Mr. Bynell to receipt for any wire traffic that comes through. He cannot do that if his fingers are broken." The runty little has-been was not looking Al in the face but had turned his head away.

"That's what you're here for," Chuck said in a bored tone. "Just in case."

"And I have tried to explain to you before," J. Kenneth said softly. "This gentleman and I use the same sequence of dots and dashes to form our letters. But that is as far as the similarity goes. The—how shall I explain this—the *rhythm* of the keying, the pauses, what we refer to as the quality of the fist . . . that is as individual as a man's own signature. If I send a message, the letters and the words will be quite correct. But any reasonably adept operator, and I assure you both, the railroad hires none but the most adept of telegraph operators, any reasonably adept operator would be able to hear a difference between my fist and his. If I am required to use the key there is the possibility, somewhat better than a remote possibility, I might add, that your plan will be detected. At least that a suspicion might occur. If you are willing to take that risk. . . ." He let his voice die and deliberately shrugged. "Naturally I shall transmit whatever messages you ask of me."

Hogue was surprised. And grateful. It was more of a defense than he ever would have expected from a man who had so obviously been defeated by life.

Chuck looked at his colleague in crime with more suspicion than fondness, certainly without any shred of respect in the look he gave the scruffy little man, but after a moment the stocky robber grunted and turned to Al. "Leave the crip's hands alone," he said. "Convince him, mind you, but leave his hands be. Maybe J. Kenneth has somethin' there after all."

A pouty expression not unlike that of a spoiled little girl who has not gotten her way crossed Al Trapp's face. But Hogue noticed that he did not give Chuck any argument.

For a brief moment Hogue thought about giving the bastard a grin just to make him mad. He sighed. There had been times, times not too very long ago, when he would have done just exactly that. And then would have waded into the three of them and maybe would have whipped them too. But those times were long gone now. The moment times like that had ended was cleared defined by a surgeon's saw. Now. . . . Hogue flexed his fingers, acutely aware for the first time of how much his livelihood depended on them now and how suddenly he could be robbed of that life, just as he had once been robbed of another and much beloved way of life. Bastards, he thought. But he kept his mouth shut and his face impassive as he thought it.

He still was determined, though. No matter what, even if it meant that Al would break his hands and turn the nimble, trained fingers into a clump of claws, even so he was not going to give in and do what they asked of him. Not now. Not and cause a head-on. He just could not do that.

While Hogue Bynell might not be much of a man any more, he thought with no small amount of satisfaction, there was still a bit of the old pride left in him. Whatever Al might come up with, Hogue intended to take it.

"Hey, Chuck," Al said. He had brightened somewhat after his bout of pique a moment before.

"Umm?"

"I just had me a thought."

"Yeah?"

"When this here job is done, what would you say to a bit o' fun over in Pueblo?"

Chuck shrugged. "Prob'ly."

"What I was thinkin', Chuck, we got this ol' broad's name on the crip's letters here. It wouldn't be much of a trick to find her. You know. Have us some fun with her. Tell her her cripped-up ol' boyfriend sent us around."

Al cupped Hogue's chin in a harshly squeezing hand and hauled it around so that Hogue was looking into Al's face.

"How does that sound to you, crip? We could have all manner o' fun with that lady friend of yours an' tell her it was you said we was welcome to it. Would you like that, crip?"

Hogue was no more impressed by that threat than Chuck seemed to be.

Shoot, Hogue thought, even a robber can only be so dumb, and even Al could not be *that* stupid. Certainly Chuck was not.

There was law in this part of the country now. A whole lot more than when Hogue had first seen it. Even so, a man could get away with very nearly anything he was strong enough or mean enough to want to get away with.

But there were some things that could get a fellow hanged or maybe flayed alive in the rankest, foulest, roughest sort of jerkwater hole-in-the-wall. And messing with a decent woman was right up at the top of that list. If Al did not know it, Chuck surely would.

If Al or anyone else laid a hand on Mabel Cutcheon or on

any other decent woman, he was a sure candidate for a hanging.

Anywhere in the country a man could pull a robbery, and there would be a posse on his trail. The possemen would have themselves a fine chase, and the whole thing would be as much of a social outing as it was an effort to regain the stolen funds. The men would have themselves a fine old time of it. And if they caught the robbers, that would be fine. If they did not, well, they would still have a good time and count it an effort well spent.

If the robbers happened to kill someone in their robbery, the chase would be more intent and more prolonged. They would give it an extra bit of effort and would be altogether more serious about the affair. But, again, they would not be devastated if they failed.

If, on the other hand, it was a molester of decent women they were after instead of some soul who had gotten into robbery and murder, why, in that case there would be no play at all within the posse. In that case they would be hard and serious and intent as hell.

In that case they likely would not come back until they had left a rope and some cottonwood fruit somewhere behind them.

Nossir, Hogue thought, old Al was not going to frighten him with that kind of threat.

Hogue looked calmly toward Chuck and ignored Al.

"Hey, Chuck."

"Umm?"

"I think I got it this time."

"Yeah?"

"For sure this time."

Chuck grunted.

"You ever visit one o' them hospitals during the war?" Al asked.

"A time or two."

"And we all seen plenty o' boys afterward hobblin' around with empty sleeves an' empty pants legs and such, right?"

The answer to that was too obvious for Chuck to bother making a reply. Everyone had seen those same pitiful sights after the war. The battlefield surgeon's principal technique for curing a shattered limb had been to cut it off. East or West, there were still a great many men who would never be sure if their enemy had been wearing a uniform with a color different from theirs or if they had been harmed the more by the medical people who had been supposed to help them.

"Right," Al answered himself. "An' d'you know what they all complain about when they're begging for drinks? Sure you do. They all of them bitch 'bout their stumps." Al took a drink and smiled. "Them ol' stumps is supposed to hurt something awful. So that there's the thing to work on." He grinned all the broader. "An' if that don't work, why, we can always give the crip here *another* stump to remember us by."

"Just so you don't mess with his hands," Chuck said. "J. Kenneth said don't mess with his hands, right?"

"Right, Chuck. I won't have to touch his hands atall."

Al left Hogue's side and headed toward his friend. He began to poke kindling into the open mouth of the potbelly stove, whistling while he went about the chore.

Hogue wondered for a moment what the man might be up to there after the threats he had just been making.

And then Hogue realized what it was that Al intended.

Hogue began to feel sick at his stomach.

CHAPTER 16

"In that box over there. No, dammit, the one in the corner. Yeah, that's it."

Al sounded positively cheerful as he crumpled some of the second-copy flimsies from Hogue's files and shoved them into the potbelly stove. He laid some split kindling sticks in on top of them and began to cram chunks of wood in on top of it all.

In the meantime Chuck was pawing through the food box Al had pointed out to him.

"There's some bacon here," Chuck said. "How does that sound to you?"

"Anything," Al told him. "My gut feels shriveled up like a raisin. Bacon's fine. See any eggs?"

The question was probably asked as a joke. Except in towns of fairly substantial size, a man could go for months without seeing an actual egg in this part of the country. But Chuck shook his head seriously in response to it.

"There's some tinned stuff," he said.

"Crackers?"

"Yeah."

"Bacon an' crackers will do," Al said. He definitely sounded cheerful now.

Hogue looked around to where Chuck was still rummaging through the box of foods. Hogue paid little attention to food himself, and he had no idea how long the slab of smoked bacon might have been in the box. For all he knew—no, for all he *hoped*—the stuff was rotten and would poison them. It was too faint a possibility to be a hope, really, but what the hell, he could always wish for it.

Hogue glared back toward Al. The fire was beginning to catch now, flame from the wadded paper licking at the dry kindling and fresh tongues of bright yellow flowing around the more solid pieces of chunked wood the line delivered to the station winter and summer for cooking as well as heating purposes.

In a short time, too short a time, those chunks of hard wood would be reduced to coals. Hogue shuddered at the thought of what a sadistic man might be able to think of with a batch of coals at his disposal. And Hogue had no doubt at all that that was exactly what Al Trapp intended.

Meanwhile the creep would cook his dinner over the same coals.

If Hogue had a gun. . . .

But he did not. That was the thing. He had no gun and no knife fit for fighting with, not even the mobility of his own broken body to fend them off with. Even his crutch, the symbol if not exactly the cause of all his problems— even that was too unwieldy to serve as a proper weapon in such close quarters.

Hogue grimaced. Oddly enough, though, his thoughts at the moment were not on what might lie ahead. He was thinking about the lousy stove and the fact that Al had started a fire in it without first cleaning it out. There would be several months of nonburnable junk accumulated in there, and Hogue would have a time cleaning it out after the ashes were cool. Hogue allowed himself to work up an anger about that and deliberately tried to ignore the other thoughts he might have been having about the fire.

J. Kenneth, for his part, shifted his crate away from the growing heat of the fire and stared studiously out the doorway toward the freer, cleaner world beyond.

Bastards, Hogue was thinking. All of them.

Al fed more wood into the now loudly drawing fresh fire while Chuck used Hogue's butcher knife to slice off several thick strips of bacon from the slab. Hogue watched the process and was not particularly surprised to see Chuck wipe the knife blade clean of the rancid grease left by the bacon and then tuck the long butcher knife between his belt and holster. Not that Hogue had really expected the man to be stupid enough to leave the knife where Hogue could grab it, but still. . . .

The four of them sat in an awkward silence while Al continued to feed the flames. The sound of the fire had settled into a dull, constant moan that seemed to fill the small shack.

Hogue looked away and licked his lips with a tongue that had gone as dry as his lips had suddenly become.

He kept thinking now about the coals that were forming inside the belly of the stove. And about the stink of burning hair and flesh that rose every time a hot iron was applied to the flank of a calf.

How many branding fires had Hogue built, and how many irons had he pressed into living flesh? He had no way to remember them all.

Now it was going to be his turn.

CHAPTER 17

There had been that time—oh, he could not even remember for sure now how long ago it had been—'way back before he ever thought about coming to this part of the country. Back in South Texas it had been, and Hogue Bynell had not been more than eighteen or nineteen years old at the time. Back when he was still trying to prove to the grown men he worked with that he was as much of a hand as they were. And that had been a long time ago indeed.

He had been working that fall for Harlan Platt down on the Frio River in that spiny, spikey, double-tough country known as the brasada.

Hogue, young Hogue, had been one of the few who had chosen to come back to Harlan after the trail drive north into Kansas that summer, and he was still rankling because he had had to ride drag and swallow dust for every one of those long miles. Now older hands who had not even gone with Platt on the drive north had been given the choice jobs of cutting the calves from the herd and heeling them with their short, heavy, rawhide reatas and dragging them to the branding fire, where other older, experienced hands were doing the actual branding. A beardless Hogue Bynell and a bunch of wet-behind-the-ears kids from neighboring outfits were assigned the lowly chore of doing the mugging.

Whenever a fresh calf was dragged close enough, it was

Hogue's job to throw it if it was still on its feet or hold it down if it had already fallen and keep it there while one of the older hands slapped the iron to it and another's knife blade flashed to notch the ears and, if it was a bull calf, castrate the bawling little beastie.

A real old timer—Hogue remembered too late and winced at the thought of how he had looked down on the old codger at the time—with a twisted, nearly useless left leg that somebody said was an injury from some long-ago battle with marauding Mexicans, had been hobbling around from fire to fire with a tin bucket of grease in his bony old hand and a cloth swab on the end of a stick. It was his job—any kid old enough to walk could have done it—to swab each fresh burn with the salted grease. Otherwise, late in the season or not, there was the danger of screwworms getting into the burn wounds. In South Texas it seemed as though there was *always* the danger of screwworms. Some years they got so bad there wasn't a ranch in the country that could feed its men rice, because the damned grains reminded everybody so of the screwworm larvae that were eating into the living cattle.

Hogue remembered that and remembered the old man—at least he had seemed old from Hogue's then-young point of view, although he might not have been any more than forty. Briefly Hogue wondered what the old fellow's name had been—he could not remember now—and whether being crippled had bothered him then as much as being one-legged bothered Hogue now.

Probably not, Hogue decided with more than a little bitterness. At least that ancient had had some sort of leg underneath him, even if it was not right. And at least he had been able to do some sort of work at the branding. For Hogue there would not even be that much. Not ever again.

But back then Hogue had been young and tall and stout of limb if not as bull-strong as he would become with his maturity. And his blood had been running hot.

He mugged calves day after day, each and every afternoon as the morning's gather was sorted and roped and dragged to the branding fires, and with every calf Hogue flanked and with every whiff of stinking hair smoke that reached his nostrils, he became angrier.

He resented the look of every older and more experienced mounted man who rode to the fire with a kicking calf at the end of his rope, and finally he had had enough.

Hogue and some downy-cheeked kid who claimed he was from England but who was probably lying about that because he talked like a damnyankee and no damnyankee in Texas at that time would ever admit to being a damnyankee—anyway, the two of them had been trying to flank a yearling heifer that had been missed in the last fall's branding and who now was big enough to be a handful for any two men, let alone one man, Hogue, and a dumb kid who did not yet know enough to wipe himself.

Hogue was having to do nearly all of the work himself, and the more he tugged and lifted and wrestled, the ranker that yearling heifer became.

She bawled and Hogue swore and both of them sweated, and after more than a minute of the standup fight—which had begun to attract some unwelcome attention from the branding crew nearby—the damnfool kid's hands had slipped and the heifer got a hind leg free just about the time Hogue was bending to try a fresh hold on the miserable beast's fore-leg, thinking he would pick her up and fling her down if he had to go down in the muck and manure with her.

As soon as that hind leg was free, the heifer used it. She humped her back and gave a little hitch to the side and let that back foot fly.

If Hogue had been standing just a little bit farther away from the lousy heifer, he would have been gumming his food for the rest of his days, and as it was her hoof caught him a glancing jolt on the chest and some part of the foot found his chin and snapped his jaws shut so hard his teeth hurt for three days after.

It knocked his hat off and bloodied his nose and stood him upright with a flush of quick anger already threatening to make his ears as red as the blood that was beginning to trickle out of his nostrils.

The heifer gave another kick that shook the damnyankee kid loose, and that freed her from the catch-man's heel rope at the same time, and she darted back for the safety of the herd that was being held by more of those older, experienced hands.

Hogue saw the heifer go and did not care a little bit. Not that there was anything a man on foot could have done to stop her anyhow.

He glared at the heifer and then at the kid who was supposed to be helping him and finally at the mounted, laughing men who were sitting their horses in comfort all around.

"All right. All *right!*" he shouted. "You think that's funny? I'll show you funny."

He picked up his hat and dusted it off against his breeches and very deliberately settled the battered old hat back where it belonged. He hitched up his pants and took his belt in a notch tighter against the activity that was about to follow.

He spit on his hands the way he had seen a professional prizefighter do once and balled his work-hardened hands into fists.

And then young Hogue Bynell proceeded to wade into that whole damned crew.

He decked the damnyankee kid with the first swing, which perhaps was not entirely fair, since the kid, who may have been English after all, was nothing like a fair match for Hogue.

Then he turned on the nearest rider and dragged the fellow down to punching level, leaving a mighty startled horse to bolt off with its saddle empty and reins dragging.

From that point it had turned into something of a free-for-all except that no one was choosing up sides. Hogue had already done that for them, and he was all there was on his side of it.

The boys on the roping horses came sailing in after him and the much older fellows working the irons backed away, and some of the hands who were supposed to be holding the gather came to add their licks, and inside of two minutes the herd was spooked and running and half the horses that were under saddle that day had gone off to join the running bovines, and the patch of cleared ground where they had been doing the branding was a mass of dust and flailing arms and hard fists so that a man couldn't see what was up and what was down.

It was a helluva mess, actually.

Hogue grunted to himself.

He wished he could remember that he had come out of that one a winner.

The truth was that he was bunged up and sore and scabbed over in more places than a poorly educated man would be able to count.

And he was out of a job, too. Spent that whole next winter shunting horses from pen to pen at the livestock market in San Antonio, because it was already too late to catch onto a riding job, a real job, anywhere in the country. Especially anywhere that might not have heard about his little fiasco down on the Frio, because there were rather few outfits, he discovered, that had not gotten the word before he showed up with his request for work to do.

Still, by damn, it had been worth it. He had showed them.

And that was the last job he ever took where he was not treated like and paid like a full-grown hand.

Hogue sighed and sat back in the swivel chair the railroad provided for him at his desk. His hand fell involuntarily toward his thigh and he reached down to massage the tender folds of neatly fitted and sewn flesh at his stump.

He had been a *man* back then, Hogue thought, and the smell of burning hair and live meat had been just part of the job that was his to do.

Now . . . he felt cold.

The smell of cooking bacon did not make his mouth water. Not this day. Now it made his stomach turn over with a queasy anticipation.

Hogue Bynell felt a growing terror that made his gut sour and brought the taste of bile to his throat.

Al Trapp was looking at him. And grinning.

CHAPTER 18

"That was a pretty good meal, crip. You should've had you some. Y' might not have much appetite later on." Al grinned again. "Unless, of course, you change your mind an' do what we need done."

Trapp did not sound as if he expected—or wanted—Hogue to change his mind.

"You really should listen to them, Mr. Bynell," J. Kenneth said.

At least, Hogue had noticed, the undersized rummy had not joined the other two in their meal. J. Kenneth had sat in silent disapproval throughout. Hogue looked his way.

"These, uh, gentlemen are quite capable of inflicting whatever pain is required to gain your compliance, Mr. Bynell. Charles will do so as a matter of perceived necessity, Alonzo as a matter of pleasure. In neither instance are you likely to benefit, Mr. Bynell. I truly suggest that you do as they wish, and the three of us will be gone in short order."

Hogue looked at the little telegrapher and set his jaw.

All that remembering, painful and otherwise, had reminded him that, by damn, once upon a time he had been willing to take on anything and anybody and damn the consequences.

He had been whipped that time down in Texas so very long ago. He had been whipped bad. He had known that when he started the fracas, had known he could not fight so many and hope to come out of it with a whole skin.

And that had been over an issue of wounded pride. If the lives of two train crews were not worth more to him than his own sensitive pride once had been, well, there would be something plain wrong with him. Wouldn't there?

Hogue assured himself that there would be something dreadfully wrong indeed if that were so.

He set his jaw and looked J. Kenneth square in the eyes. He shook his head slowly from side to side.

Al Trapp had been watching the exchange. Now the outlaw laughed, and Hogue did not like the sound of Al's laughter.

"You'll do what we want," Al said. He sounded . . . different from before. There was some new quality in the man's voice, and for a moment Hogue had trouble trying to decide what it was.

Finally he got it. Trapp sounded almost . . . *nice*. Almost pleasant. It was as if there were a bond of affection between Al and Hogue now.

Al Trapp had something seriously wrong with him, Hogue decided. Seriously wrong.

But even so, he could not now transmit that train order. Not when it would mean the loss of life. At the very least it would have to mean that. At the very least the engine crews on the trains would be killed. Maybe some brakemen as well.

No, Hogue thought, he could not do that. Not to anyone, not even to trainmen.

But it surely was a lousy position he had been put in here. He looked at J. Kenneth and shrugged. The rummy looked away.

"No need to wait, is there?" Al asked. He was directing the question to Chuck.

The blocky straw boss shook his head. "No, but remember what J. Kenneth said. Don't touch his hands. Do whatever else you got to, but leave his hands be. We might be needing those."

"Whatever you want," Al said cheerfully.

Al tossed his tin plate and the fork he had been eating with into the now empty woodbox with a clatter. He was done with the utensils and obviously did not care about them any further. If anyone cleaned up his mess, it would have to be Hogue.

Hogue glared at the man. It was no consolation at all that the two must have had a terrible meal. The fire Al had built had been roaringly hot when they were cooking on it. Entirely too hot for the purpose of cooking. But now it had died somewhat and there would be a deep bed of cherry-red coals left in the stove. That, after all, had been Al's primary purpose in building the fire. The food had been an afterthought.

Hogue was still hoping the both of them would curl up with the miseries in their bellies from the elderly bacon or from rat poison or from some unseen hand of justice or. . . . Or from anything, really.

Not that he expected it. It would just be nice if it were to happen.

It was just as well that Hogue was not expecting anything like that, because it did not happen.

Al stood and belched with contentment and rubbed his now full stomach and smiled pleasantly at Hogue. "Reckon you should get yourself ready, ol' crip."

Hogue sat where he was, frightened but still determined

that he would *not* write out the falsified train order that they demanded.

Al approached him and reached down to touch Hogue's shoulder. "You wanta lie down on the desk there by yourself or should I plant you there myself?"

Hogue kicked him.

Al might have forgotten that a one-legged man still does have one leg left for kicking purposes, at least when he is sitting down.

Hogue planted his one remaining foot in Al Trapp's crotch.

Al squealed like a knife-stuck hog and jumped back.

Hogue knew at once that the reaction was out of proportion to the small amount of damage he had been able to do. The chair seat was too low and the angle too far off for him to get a square hit on the target. But Al acted initially as if it had been the most devastating blow ever struck.

Unfortunately that response did not last very long. A moment later, Trapp had regained his composure.

Any trace of pleasantness, feigned or real, was gone from the man's face now. He looked as though he was ready to kill Hogue with his bare hands. He took a step forward and then another. Hogue shut his eyes and tried not to cringe away from him.

CHAPTER 19

Hogue Bynell had been pounded on many and many a time before, by horse and cow and human hand, but this was something else indeed.

He hurt as he did not know it was possible to hurt. It was worse by far than the break that had eventually taken his leg, even worse than when the leg was long broken and rotting.

For the past little while—he had no idea how long it had been going on although he thought, rather dispiritedly, that it had not really been nearly as long as it seemed—he had been drifting in and out of consciousness.

He was reasonably certain that he could remember hearing Chuck order Al not to injure his hands or his head, probably to make sure there would be no brain damage that would make him useless to them. And he had an impression that J. Kenneth had been saying something, or maybe yelling something, a time or two as well. He was not sure.

About the only thing he was sure of, certain-sure of, was that he hurt like hell.

And Trapp was not even using anything on him except his bare hands.

All the choice little tricks and twists were still to come. Irons or coals or whatever, none of that had yet been applied.

For that matter, Al had not yet bothered to ask if Hogue was willing to give in and write out the train order.

That would come later, probably, but for the moment Al seemed interested only in extracting a measure of personal revenge for the kick Hogue had launched at the outlaw's cods.

One thing anyway, Hogue thought drunkenly. At least so far the only thing Hogue Bynell was sorry for about that kick was that he had not been on target better than he was.

He rolled his head and looked up at Al—somehow, Hogue was not sure when, he had been picked up and thrown onto his back atop the broad work surface of his desk—and tried to give the man a nasty grin. He did not really know if he had managed the expression but he felt somewhat better for having tried.

Some of it must have gotten through anyway. Al redoubled his efforts, and this time he apparently forgot Chuck's warnings because his blows from a hammered fist began to fall on Hogue's head and face.

In a way, that was quite nice. Almost immediately, the pain Hogue was feeling lessened, and he began to feel himself slide down a long, gray chute toward a sort of warm, soft darkness.

Pain.

Hell, pain was practically an old friend. Certainly it was an acquaintance of very long standing.

Pain could be a part of any day when you rode rank horses and fought wild cattle for your living.

It did not have to come from trying to make a living either. It could come as well from a man's play.

There had been that time—Hogue's thoughts and his recall were totally clear on the subject, and for the time being he was able to escape whatever it was that Al person was doing to him—when Hogue and Goodnight Licken and a Y Knot rider named Coy Forrest asked for some time off and rode all the way over to the mountains on a hunt.

They told the boss man they were going after elk, which made it all right on several counts. One would be that while the three of them were off playing they would not be drawing pay from the outfit. The other was that if they brought back a few packhorses loaded with elk meat it would go toward their winter supplies and the outfit would have another cull or two to sell come spring. So it was all right with the boss.

The truth was that Coy was even crazier than Hogue and Goodnight, and had it in his head that he was going to find a grizzly bear up in those high mountains and was going to dab a rope onto the thing. Hogue and Goodnight were just crazy enough that they wanted to go along and watch, so the three of them cooked up the story for the foreman and took off with the outfit's blessings and a string of Y Knot horses.

That had been a fine ride, Hogue remembered. The high country was already being filled with miners in the spots where discoveries had been made, but there was so *much* country up there that even a loony bunch like those miners were could not fill it and ruin it, no matter how hard they tried.

The three of them had trailed their string up the Arkansas to the place where the river flow filled the bottom of a sheer, rock-walled gorge that must have been a mile high above the level of the river—well, that was an exaggeration maybe, but not much of one—and they had had to turn aside.

They rode north from there, ambling in no particular direction and no particular hurry up one canyon and over another ridge, and from every high place it seemed as if they could see even farther than they had seen from the one before.

The country was different up there. Lots of trees. Lots of rocks. Not much grass although enough to feed a hobbled horse. And mostly the ground ran to up-and-down rather than north-and-south.

It was not really a cattleman's sort of country, but Hogue liked it anyway. He liked being able to top out one of those high, rocky, wind-barren ridges with the few scraggly junipers all twisted and shaggy and being able to see the saw-toothed white of distant mountain ranges that might have been as little as fifty or as much as a hundred miles away. And more waves of peaks in between.

A man's heart gets a peculiar kind of lift when he sits on a horse on a mountaintop with the whole wide world spread out at his feet.

So, yes, Hogue had really enjoyed that trip, and he had an idea that Goodnight and Coy enjoyed it too, although of course they did not discuss any of that. There are some schoolteacherish thoughts that a man likes to keep private.

They were enjoying the trip, but they were not finding any bear or even much in the way of elk. There were enough mule deer to keep them from being hungry but not much else, so they kept going.

A few days out from the river, they climbed into a high mountain valley of decent grass surrounded by mountains, the sort of place the old timers used to call a "park" up in this part of the country, and there they began to pick up signs of more and better game.

In particular there was bear sign. Droppings and clawed

trees and what Coy Forrest claimed quite seriously was a "feel" of bear in the area. Coy claimed to be something of an expert on that subject, although Hogue wondered, if the fellow was so much of an all-fired expert, why he hadn't gotten around to roping a bear before then.

At any rate, neither Hogue nor Goodnight particularly cared, and if Coy wanted to stop, that was all right by them. They made their camp on a broad, grassy meadow beside a thin, cold stream and hung a few bells around the necks of their packhorses before they hobbled the animals and turned them loose. A hobbled horse can cover an amazing amount of territory in a single night's time, and a smart one can manage to hide behind a lone aspen sapling if you do not string a bell on him to make him give himself away.

There seemed to be no roads or mines or even prospectors in the park, and while white men had undoubtedly been through the area a thousand times in the past fifty years, Hogue liked to privately suppose to himself that the three of them were the first humans who had set foot in that area since the last Indian tribe moved out.

Hogue and Goodnight would have been content to lie up along the sides of the creek to soak up some sunshine and sleep through the lazy afternoons and maybe try to snag a few trout, but Coy would not have it that way.

There were bear around, he kept insisting, and big grizzlies at that, and he wanted one of those rascals and would have one or his name was not Coy Forrest.

Neither Hogue nor Goodnight would really have cared if Coy had decided to change his name, but they had come to see the man rope a grizzly and so they would go along with him now.

The thing to do, Coy told them, was for the three of them to split up and go in three separate directions looking for fresh bear sign.

Once they spotted a good place that a really big grizz was using, they would all come back together, and Coy would have his chance to do his roping. Hogue and Goodnight would act as his hazers to run the bear near his rope, and then it would be all over for old Mr. Silvertip.

As far as Hogue was concerned, it was all just a good excuse to ride out and see more country, and that was all right by him whether or not they ever saw a bear. At least up in this park they could count on finding some elk and they would still have jobs when they got back down onto the big grass, where a cow's legs did not have to grow with one side short and the other side long for hillside grazing.

The first day out, neither Hogue nor Goodnight reported seeing the first lick of bear sign, but Coy swore up and down that he had spotted some telltales to the north and east of their camp, so that was the area they would all search the next day.

That might have been believable enough except that Coy also told them that he had roped a yearling elk that very afternoon but had not killed it, as it would not have provided enough meat to be worth the bother. If Hogue had really cared about what they were supposed to be doing on their trip, he might have started to get annoyed with Coy by that time, but he did not and so let it pass unchallenged.

At any rate, the three of them rode out to the northeast the next morning and followed the creek for a few miles before they split up.

Coy gave himself the "beariest"-looking area to search,

which was due east. Goodnight rode north. And Hogue split the line between them, following a bend in the creek toward a huge, dome-shaped rock that he had been admiring ever since they had topped the last rise and gotten it in view.

For some reason, Hogue was quite taken with that dome of slick rock, and he got it in mind that he would like to see the lay of the country from up on top of that thing.

He rode straight for it, ignoring half a dozen herds of mule deer and a small band of cow elk even though he had a borrowed carbine slung under his leg and could have taken home some meat if he had wanted. Instead he wanted to climb up that rock, illogical as that was and in spite of the fact that it was plain from a long ways back that no horse was ever going to make that climb. If he did it, it would have to be afoot.

Hogue reached the base of the dome by late morning and found that, up close, the rock was both a whole lot bigger than he had expected and a whole lot less smoothly formed.

Down around the base, it was jagged enough to make a goat fretful, and some places it looked as if it would take a healthy bird to make it from one handhold to the next.

Still, Hogue had set his mind to it, and he intended to get to the top.

He rode around the base a little, casting back and forth for the most likely-looking spot to begin his crawl, and finally he just said the hell with it. He slipped down out of his saddle, loosened his cinches and tied the horse to a picket pin so he would know for damn sure the animal would be there when he got back. He had no desire at all to walk back to camp and take a hazing from the others when he and his horse came in separately.

Full of determination, Hogue began to climb.

He did all right for the first fifty feet or so, but that was hardly a good start on the job he had set for himself. Then his luck changed.

He was reaching for a handhold far overhead when his slick-soled riding boots slipped and his feet shot out from under him.

Hogue's head bounced off a rock harder than any calf is able to kick and bounced off a second rock even harder.

He slid nearly half the distance he had been able to climb, fell free off a narrow ledge to the next-outward hump of hard rock and slid the rest of the way down to the gravelly soil and sparse grass of the relatively flat land at the bottom of the rock dome.

When he came to, his scalp was laid open across the right side of his head, his left ankle was badly twisted and probably sprained, and he was scraped bloody raw over a large share of his body surface.

To say he was in agony then would have been a masterpiece of understatement. It would have been far enough short of the mark to be considered a lie, much like calling Grant a social tippler on rare occasion.

There was nothing on, in or about Hogue that had not hurt then.

Yet he had been able to grit his teeth and cuss himself for a damn fool, then crawl back to his horse, undo the stubborn knot he had put into the picket rope, tighten his cinches and take himself back to camp in time to be there when the others rode in to report on their day's findings or lack thereof.

That and the few days afterward had been just about all

the pain Hogue thought there could be in a single human body.

Until now.

Now that fall and the healing period afterward seemed about as painful as a mashed thumb, at least in comparison, and Hogue would gladly have gone through it twice again if it would convince Al Trapp to lay off of him now.

He groaned and tried to bite back the sound and could not help thinking about Coy Forrest. Hogue had heard that old Coy broke his neck down in Arizona Territory while he was trying to rope a javelina pig.

Hogue wondered if Coy had ever gotten a chance to put a rope on a bear. Any sort of bear. Hogue kind of hoped that he had, although it sure had not happened on the trip they had taken together that time.

And, no, Hogue Bynell was damned well *not* going to give in to these creeps and write out the train order they wanted. No way.

CHAPTER 20

"Back off, Al."

"What?"

"You've played with him long enough," Chuck said. "We aren't here for that, we're here to do a job. It's time you get down to it."

Trapp looked disappointed. But he did not argue. He stood up—he had been bent over Hogue's supine position atop the hard and now sweat-slick surface of the railroad-issue desk—and turned away.

Hogue lay there with the pain a constant boil deep in his gut and felt a slim measure of pride returning. He had taken Al Trapp's punishment and he had not broken and that was much to be thankful for. And proud of. There had been little enough in recent years that he could point to with any satisfaction. So maybe he was one-legged but not as totally worthless as he had been thinking. Maybe there was still something left of the man he once had been. Maybe. . . .

Trapp was returning to the desk now.

The son of a bitch was carrying, rather gingerly, a small shovel.

Hogue recognized the shovel. It was the little pressed-tin scoop Hogue used from time to time to clean the ashes out of the stove.

The shovel was smoldering. Or, rather, small wisps of

smoke were rising from it. Hogue lifted his head and strained his neck to see, although he did not really *want* to see. He already knew what the shovel contained.

"Strip his breeches off," Al ordered.

Chuck and now even J. Kenneth moved to help.

Hogue felt them fumbling with his belt, felt the buckle being tugged tighter and then quickly falling free, felt strange hands opening the buttons at his fly. He had become almost used to having others handle and dress and clean him when he was in the makeshift hospital that time. Now . . . this was different. Now the feeling was terrifying.

The men stripped his trousers from his hips and left him lying there chilly and exposed in a way that went far beyond the physical sensations he was experiencing.

Hogue gathered what strength he had left after the beating Al had so effectively administered.

He tried to lash out at them. Tried to roll away and flail his arms and fight them off.

He had neither the strength nor the leverage. Chuck held him down on one side and J. Kenneth on the other, and Hogue was powerless to resist them.

For the first time in . . . for the first time ever, really, he regretted the loss of weight and muscle he had undergone since his accident. There had been a time when— That time was long past. He could do nothing to help himself now. It no longer mattered what once was or what might have been, and Hogue understood that but was unable to stop himself from regretting it.

"Bastards," he hissed at them.

They ignored him.

Trapp used a free hand to complete the brief task of pulling Hogue's shortened and sewed-off pants leg from his stump, allowing the trousers to dangle from Hogue's one remaining leg.

Hogue felt a wave of shame flood through him when Al Trapp looked at the bare, exposed, almost flat knob where Hogue's leg so abruptly ended.

The flesh there was acutely tender.

Flaps of living skin and meat had been left below the point where the bone and muscle were severed and forever taken from him.

Those flaps had been folded and snipped and fitted with a seamstress's care and sewn into place.

Until now only the doctor and Hogue himself had seen them.

Now Al Trapp looked at the stump with dispassionate interest, and Hogue felt the sense of shame grow, felt his face heat up and knew that he was reddening with the embarrassment of it.

The embarrassment was worse than the pain of the physical beating had ever become.

Hogue wanted to turn his head away, would have hidden if he could, but his eyes were locked on the contents of the small shovel with a will of their own.

There were coals in the scoop of the tin shovel. Coals from the fire Al and Chuck had cooked their lunch over. The coals glowed a pulsing red heat that demanded Hogue's attention.

"They say it's awful tender down there," Al said cheerfully. "This is your chance, crip. Speak up now an' you'll be just fine. Do what we ask an' we'll put these li'l red apples right back into the firebox over there. It's up t' you, crip. Just do what we ask."

"He'll do it, you know," Chuck said. "And we can get along without you if we must. You won't accomplish anything by making us do this. Give in, man."

Hogue bit his lip and squeezed his eyes shut. He shook his head.

He had his pride—some of it—left to him. He could not give in now. He would not do it.

"Please," J. Kenneth pleaded in a soft voice. "Do as they want. Please, Mr. Bynell."

Hogue shook his head.

His eyes were closed but he could hear Al Trapp's short bark of pleased laughter. He could visualize the wolf-like grin that would be on the sadistic bastard's face even if he could not see it. He did not have to see it to know it was there.

"I can't," Hogue whispered. His voice, he discovered, had become hoarse.

The reasons for his refusal hardly mattered any more. The reasons no longer had much to do with the two trains that would collide if he gave in, nor with the men who would die if the false order was sent.

Now it had become a matter of simple pride to Hogue Bynell.

He had not really known he had anything left of a man's pride.

Now that he had discovered a remnant of manhood inside himself, he wanted to keep it. It was much, much more than he had known he had. He wanted to hold onto it and know it was there.

"Go to hell," Hogue said. He was pleased to hear that this time his voice was firm. "You won't get nothing from me today, boys." He would have given them a manful laugh of defiance too, but he could not manage that.

He lay back and waited.

He had taken pain before. He had endured everything that had been thrown at him. He would endure this too.

He was sure of that.

He heard a movement from the direction where Al Trapp had been standing, heard the scrape of a boot sole on the wooden floor, felt a hand on his thigh above the stump, a firm hold placed there.

It would be coming now, and—

Hogue screamed.

The sound was torn unwillingly from his throat.

Under and through the terrible noise of his scream, Hogue could hear the sizzle of his own scorched and burning flesh. He could smell a sudden odor of braised meat.

"STOP!!!"

His body bucked and contorted under the restraining hands of the men who were holding him pinned to the desk top.

"For God's sake stop."

Hogue heard himself begin to whimper.

"Anything. I'll do anything you say."

Hogue Bynell loathed himself. Disgust for his own weakness rolled through him like cold water entering a drowning man's lungs.

"Anything," he whimpered. "I'll do what you want. Just stop."

CHAPTER 21

Hogue sat slumped in his railroad-issue swivel chair, his mind numb and uncaring.

It did not seem to matter at all, now, that he had done what they wanted of him. He had written out their train order in his precise, careful hand, using the correct form and the correct wording and doing it exactly as Chuck and Al and J. Kenneth wished.

That did not seem to matter now and neither did much of anything else.

Hogue sat with his trousers pulled back up where they belonged and his fly more or less buttoned but with his belt unbuckled and dangling from the first and last loops at his waist. That did not matter either. The others had seen his stump, so what could an unbuckled belt matter anyway?

They had also seen Hogue Bynell crumple as completely and as uselessly as a child in the grip of the night terrors.

So how could it matter even that they had seen and had abused his stump?

Next to that, the physical deformity was as nothing.

An hour before, Hogue would have been shocked by that thought. Now it seemed quite perfectly plain.

Now that it was too late, that is. Now the damage had been done.

Hogue felt . . . empty. A rusted bucket with a rotted-out hole in the bottom, of no use to anyone for any purpose.

He had felt bad before. He thought he had discovered how low a man can feel back when he awakened and for the first time saw that flat, level, empty expanse of sheet where his leg had been.

That was almost laughable now, realizing the feelings he had had then and how wrong he had been.

At least then, if he had not been a complete man, he had at the very least been a human being who might still retain some shreds of pride.

Now. . . . There would be none of that now. There could not be anything left to be proud of now.

Oh, he had been so damnably proud and brave and convinced of his own resolve, hadn't he?

You bet, he told himself.

Until that first touch of a coal to his flesh. And then the screaming and the crying and the giving in.

Sure, it was perfectly all right that a pair of unsuspecting trains smash into each other head-on. It would be perfectly all right for half a dozen men to be smashed along with them. So what about a little thing like that? Hogue would not have to be there to see it happen. It would just be a flash of news along the wire when someone discovered it, when one of the trains failed to show up on schedule and someone was sent to investigate. It would just be a rumor by then, just so much talk.

Hogue would never have to look at the blood or listen to the screams of pain or see the globs of gray and red and white splattered amid the wreckage. Maybe some poor bastard of a trainman would have his leg crushed and have it amputated. So what? Hogue would never have to face him about it.

And all that was all right. Obviously. Just so good old Hogue Bynell did not have to stand a little pain. *Jesus!*

Hogue sickened himself.

He sat staring sightlessly toward the floor, uncaring what might be going on around him in the small shack, despising himself as a coward and worse.

And when the key clattered into noisy life beside him, Hogue reached for it without thinking and began to accept the incoming message. Just exactly as he knew they would want him to do. Exactly as they asked of him. So he would not again incur their displeasure. So they would hurt him no more.

That, after all, was the only thing that seemed to have any remote interest or acceptability now.

There simply was nothing else left for him.

CHAPTER 22

"Let me see that." Trapp took a quick step toward him.

Hogue flinched away in a sudden grip of renewed fear, but all Al did was snatch the message form from Hogue's unresisting fingers. Al peered at the form and seemed to be puzzling over it. Hogue realized that the man could read poorly if at all. Not that it mattered. Very little seemed to matter any more.

"It's routine stuff," Hogue mumbled.

Neither Al nor Chuck was willing to accept his statement. They looked to J. Kenneth for confirmation.

"He told you the truth," the little man said. "Let him relay it on if you do not want to raise suspicions."

Trapp glowered at Hogue. "Make sure you send it straight, then. Ol' J. Kenneth will be listenin'."

Hogue did not bother to answer. There was, after all, nothing he could say. He bent to his key, threw the relay switches and began repeating the transmission for the benefit of the next station down the line.

When he was done he noticed, somewhat fearfully, that Trapp had wandered behind him again and was again pawing through his private things. Hogue tried to pay no attention, but in truth he was aware of every motion Al Trapp made behind him. Any movement might signal another blow.

Trapp was prowling through the metal box again, the one where Mabel Cutcheon's letters had been stored.

"You know, crip," Al said cheerfully, "you're really just about worthless, ain't you? No good to this here woman. No good to the railroad. Jus' no good at all. Ain't you?"

"That's right," Hogue agreed dully. "No good at all." He was not now agreeing with Trapp for the sake of expedience. It was, he thought, the simple truth. He was no good at all, not to anyone.

And, he thought to himself, maybe the bastard could not read well, but he could read to some extent. And more's the pity, Hogue thought. He squeezed his eyes shut.

Mabel Cutcheon had been one of the good things that had happened to him in the past, but now that possibility was gone as completely as his leg.

The simple things had been . . . nice . . . back before the accident, after her husband died, when Hogue would come into town on those rare occasions, feeling tired from the hard work of riding and working cattle and fighting bad horses, physically tired but nevertheless feeling strong and fit and capable of very nearly anything.

Then he and the widow lady might have a bite of dinner, much better than anything to be found in a line camp or burnt over a solitary fire made from dried cow chips in those broad, barren, thoroughly delightful stretches where there was no wood to build a fire with but only dried grasses and dung and whatever else a man might be able to scrounge.

They might eat in the widow's kitchen, a pleasant meal much less solitary than those Hogue was used to, or they might once in a great while eat in one of the decent public restaurants of the town, with Hogue standing treat and taking pride in being able to squire a woman out in public like that where everyone would see them and know that this big hulk of a hardworking male was able to find company that he did not have to pay for and that he had the wherewithal to pay for their meals at the inflated prices such restaurants charged, sometimes as much as a dollar a meal although it was very rare indeed when they might choose a place so fancy.

Still, those times had been a source of pleasure for Hogue. He had felt a sense of pride then, a sense of worth.

Now. . . .

Now those days were gone, right along with very nearly everything else Hogue Bynell had known and cared about.

Now there was nothing else left that Hogue could take pride in. Nothing. Not even the tiny spark of satisfaction he might have been able to gain from doing a good job for the railroad.

He squeezed his eyes shut even tighter.

It was odd, he reflected, that he had not even known that he was able to take any pride in his job.

Sitting at a desk with a pair of crutches propped against the wall beside him and fiddling with a damned electromagnetic key was not what he had ever considered to be a man's job. It was not like working cattle or breaking horses or getting a *real* job done no matter what man and predator and Nature might throw against him. It was a far cry from that.

But he had done it well.

He had a reputation, he knew, of never making mistakes. Of keeping his section safe. Of always being there when he was needed.

Funny that that had never meant anything to him.

And now that was ended too.

After this day, Hogue Bynell would have the reputation of an operator whose section had been the scene of disaster.

He would be an operator who had allowed a collision on the line.

Worse, he would be known as an operator who had *caused* a collision.

Oh, the others on the line might not say anything to him about it. There would be the excuse of duress. Al and Chuck and J. Kenneth would be known about.

But Hogue knew good and well that that would not make any real difference to the other relay operators or to the train crews who would pass through in the future.

They would look at Hogue and he would be able to see in their eyes the accusations even if they were never spoken.

Each and every man who passed through Relay 12 in the future would know, absolutely *know* that in Hogue Bynell's place *he* would have done something different. *He* would not have caved in to them. *He* would not have allowed, much less have caused, a wreck on the line.

But not old Hogue. No, not him. He went right ahead and let the head-on happen. But then, what could you expect from a useless damned cripple? The line ought to fire him. For that matter, Hogue thought, maybe the line *would* fire him.

Then where would he be?

What could a one-legged man do to provide for himself? Swamp saloons? Roll over and wait to die? Or just take a shortcut, buy or borrow a pistol and put a welcome slug through his own temple?

That might be the best answer after all, Hogue thought.

Hell, it wasn't like there would be any loss. Not to anyone. Not to the line. Not to Mabel Cutcheon. Certainly not to Hogue Bynell.

That just might be the best answer, Hogue thought.

It might be the best answer possible. Save himself a lot of pain. Save the line the trouble of firing him. Save Mabel Cutcheon the bother of her pity. Undeserved pity at that.

Hogue Bynell was not worth pitying. He knew that. He was not even worth that much.

Jesus!

He wondered if he should look for a way to do it now or if he should wait.

Waiting probably would be better, he decided. If he tried it now, he would have to make a grab for Al's gun or for Chuck's. They would probably think he was up to something and would hurt him again. Certainly they would stop him.

No, he thought, it would be better to wait. He had more than enough money on account with the line to pay for a pistol.

Any old gun would be good enough, he thought. He did not even have to buy a good one. It would only have to fire one time. Any old two-dollar castoff would be good enough for his needs.

In a way, that thought pleased him. Not even good enough to justify the purchase of a good gun. That was justice for you, he thought. Not even good enough to be worth a good gun.

He might have wept except that he knew he was not worth his own damned tears.

Jesus! The unspoken thought was more plea than exclamation.

CHAPTER 23

It had not been such a bad life, Hogue thought.

Oddly, he no longer felt any bitterness or even much in the way of depression. All that was past. All the necessary decisions had been made. Now he felt . . . contented. Reasonably so, at any rate.

And it really had not been such a bad life.

He remembered that first job, so long ago now, that first drive up the long trail from Texas across the Indian Nations to Kansas. It had been exciting, even if he had been going along as a wet-behind-the-ears young un. Appropriately so, he realized now, because that was exactly what he had been back then.

He had lied about his age in order to get the job, but he doubted now that he had fooled anyone, least of all old Mr. I. P. Conroe, who must have been in his mid-fifties at the time but who had seemed immeasurably ancient to a gangly, wild-haired boy fresh off a Missouri farm.

There was a freedom and independence in the cow business and among cowmen that said that all men were at least the equals of all others and that no son of a bitch deserved the title "mister." By rights it should have been IP or Connie or some nickname that Mr. Conroe was called, but the man had had a sort of innate dignity about him that led even the most experienced and the roughest of the hands to call him

Mr. Conroe, although there were probably not a dozen other men on earth who would have gotten that title of respect from any of them in a face-to-face conversation. With Mr. Conroe it had simply seemed the natural and proper thing to do.

Hogue smiled to himself, remembering the old gentleman.

Always neatly attired, wearing suit coat and vest, collar and tie in the midst of the dust and shouting and confusion of the loading pens or out in the middle of the big grass several days' ride from any place that might charitably be termed a civilized location. No matter what, Mr. Conroe was always dressed in a manner fit to greet a lady in, from the brim of his brushed hat to the knee-tall boots with his trouser legs tucked into their high tops and the gleam of wax polish showing under the dust.

He had been quite a man, old Mr. Conroe, and Hogue owed him a great deal for having swallowed a green kid's lies without a hint of disbelief and hired him to do a job in spite of his obvious inexperience.

Hogue sighed.

That first job had not been much: hey-boy for the cook. They had not been three days out of Kerrville when the night-hawk, who was two years older than Hogue, decided he was homesick for his mama and accepted the shame of being a quitter in order to ask for his wages and start his long walk back home.

They had needed another night herder to replace him, and Hogue had boldly asked for the job. Swore he was a rider and the very next thing to a top hand and could handle that or any other job the trail boss might put onto him. This even though the only riding he had ever been able to do in his life was on the broad back of a draft horse going from field to harness shed and back again, that and an occasional brief excursion aboard one of the milk cow's weanling calves, occasions that had rarely lasted long enough for Hogue's father to catch him at it and whale him for disturbing the stock.

That lie had probably been as easily detectable as Hogue's others, but old Mr. Conroe had given his trail boss the wink and a nod and Hogue was given a riding job—of sorts.

For the rest of that trip, Hogue remembered, he had had to pay for his lies, because the men took him at his word.

He could do any and every thing they threw at him? Fine. He could night-herd the remuda of horses *and* help the cook gather wood and water at every meal stop.

At least the men had had the decency to give him fairly gentle horses those first few days, but the gentlest of a trail string was none too gentle, and the Conroe remuda was no exception to the rule. Hogue learned to stay on by falling off, and by the time they reached Ellsworth that summer he was no longer falling off so often and they were no longer bothering to give him a gentled animal once the herd was settled and it was time for the kid from Missouri to leave the fire, bolt a quick meal and take over the responsibility of herding the horses through the long, dark and sometimes scary nights of the open country.

Hogue reflected afterward that he probably did not sleep more than three hours on any given day during the two months it took them to reach the Kansas shipping point, and that small amount of rest had to be grabbed on the run, so to speak, as he bounced and rattled around in the back of the cook's bed trailer hitched behind the wagon.

It was a wonder he had survived it, Hogue thought later,

but in the ignorance of youth he had thought it all quite grand.

Oh, it had been nothing at all like what the wild tales and his limited reading had led him to believe.

There were no stampedes to sound like thunder across the rolling plains. Nothing remotely like that. This was a market herd, after all, and old Mr. Conroe had been too wise a man to mix culled cows in with his beef for such a long trip. The entire herd, several thousand strong, was made up of mature steers, and those steers had already experienced very nearly everything that Nature could show them. They plodded forward day after day in a mile-long thin trickle of slowly moving meat on the hoof, pausing to snatch a mouthful of grass here or to take a drink there. The herders did not so much drive them as control their drift in a desired direction so that at the end of the drive the steers would be heavier and in better condition than when they left Texas.

That kind of herding was hardly exciting. Dusty, hot and boring, yes, but hardly exciting.

Still, Hogue had loved it.

He had heard stories about attacks by wild Indians, too, but he did not understand where those tales might have originated.

Oh, they saw Indians along the route. When they passed through the Nations, which was for a major portion of the trip, every so often a band of blanket-wrapped Indians would come by. But they were not there to fight. They came to beg for food or offer their women for sale or demand a toll in edible beef, and they left behind them no wounds more serious than a louse bite.

Nor were the hands Hogue rode and worked with festooned with revolvers and daggers the way Hogue had been led to believe they must always be.

Old Mr. Conroe was one of those who believed that the causes of temperance and good will were enhanced by the elimination of temptation. Neither firearms nor liquor was allowed on the drive, although Hogue happened to know, due to his association with the cook, that a jug of sour-mash whiskey and a Spencer repeating rifle were kept in the wagon. The whiskey was there in case of need for genuine medicinal purposes, and the rifle was present so that a broken-legged animal might be humanely destroyed if that became necessary. Neither had to be used on that first drive north.

Hogue had heard too about the extremes of weather that might be encountered on the drives, but those he had to wait until later years to experience for himself. On that first drive, he learned that the summer days are hot and that when it rained one became wet. On the other hand, rain settled the dust for the next day or two, so there was a benefit even in that.

They fought no enemies and forded no floods, they merely moved slowly forward for day after day under a sky that seemed too big for half a dozen worlds to contain and across limitless miles of undulating grasslands. And they moved as free men, with no fences to contain them or rules to bind them.

That was the thing. The men were as free as the country, and it was a life that Hogue loved. One that he expected to claim as his own for as long as he lived.

He sighed.

He had almost managed it too.

Almost.

He had managed it for a long, long time. That would just have to be enough.

And, really, it had been a good life.

He thought back on it fondly, and for the first time since he had awakened to that prairie-flat expanse of empty sheet where his leg had been he was content with what had been and accepting of what was to come.

It had not been such a bad life, Hogue thought.

CHAPTER 24

And this was not a time to be feeling sad or unhappy or down on himself, Hogue thought.

As a matter of fact, he did not. Not any more. He felt better than he had in— He could not remember how long now.

There had been such *good* times.

He chuckled softly to himself. He remembered the first time he had ever been chapped. Not the last, it hadn't been, but it was the first.

It was on his second drive north, nighthawking for Dave and Cletus Morgan from Beeville and thinking he was plumb experienced after one completed drive and a winter of mavericking at a dollar a head in the brasada for a group of men who called themselves the McMullen County Stockmen's Association.

Yes, he had been experienced enough, all right.

Experienced enough now to doze for short catnaps in the saddle while his night horse carried him along with the remuda and to let the horse's change of motion wake him if anything happened.

Experienced enough to give the cook's hey-boy hell whenever the kid—he was seven months younger than Hogue and on his very first drive—did something in a way other than Hogue would have done it.

Experienced enough to get his dander up and come back

with some smartass remark whenever one of the regular hands did or said something that experienced old Hogue thought was beneath him.

Oh, he had been a real pistol on that trip, Hogue thought ruefully.

Was a pistol and carried one too. After all, he was tough and experienced and practically grown-up. If the rusted and decidedly inexpensive thing did not fire more than one time in three pops of the cap through its pitted and dirt-clogged chamber nipples, well, that hardly mattered. The point was that Hogue was grown-up enough to carry a gun if he felt like it, and no one was going to tell him different.

Not that anyone tried. The Morgan brothers were looser with their crews than old Mr. Conroe had been and never tried to tell their men what to do unless it concerned their cattle. And even then they expected a man to know what needed doing and get it done without being told.

The rest of the crew put up with Hogue's overstuffed breeches and excessively tight hatband for quite a while, actually. They gave him room to run in, and run he did, bossing the hey-boy and swaggering around the fire with his dollar-fifty cap-and-ball gun on his belt and generally acting like an idiot.

The end of that period of his life started when smartmouth Hogue saw the hey-boy, whose name was Jimmy something —Hogue could no longer remember the rest of it—grab a kettle of sonuvabitch stew off the fire when the concoction, which no two cooks ever seemed to make the same way, started to boil over.

Hogue knew good and well from firsthand experience why the kid cared if the kettle boiled over. The loss of a little juice and maybe some floating dried peas would do no harm at all, but if the stuff burnt onto the outside of the cast-iron kettle, it would mean some hard, long scrubbing, which Jimmy would have to do, before the cook would be satisfied with the thing again. So naturally Jimmy wanted to avoid the problem before it occurred.

At any rate, when the mess began to run over the side of the kettle, the kid grabbed for the bail and yanked it aside to cool a bit before it might be set back onto a less hot section of coals.

Naturally enough, the metal bail of a boiling pot is going to be close to the temperature of the kettle itself, and Jimmy did not take time to go fetch a rag from the wagon tongue to protect his hand. Of course if he had waited to get the rag the kettle would have gone on boiling over and the damage would have been done; he would have had some difficult scrubbing to do, which was what he was trying to avoid in the first place.

Hogue knew this as well as Jimmy did, and the season before, he might have done exactly the same thing. This year was different, though, and Hogue did not have to act as any man's hey-boy. So when Jimmy yelped and began blowing on his hand after the kettle was safely off the fire, Hogue set in to laughing and pointing.

"You're about the dumbest kid I ever seen, Jimmy-boy. I swear you are. Listen, you ain't handling any of the food, are you? I mean, you don't actually touch anything that us working men has got to put into our mouths, do you? Because, I swear, I think you're likely too damned dumb to wipe yourself proper. I'm scared you might be gettin' something nasty onto the food, kid. I worry about that. I really do."

Hogue said that and laughed and stamped his right boot a few times in his mirth and laughed some more at the misery that was showing in Jimmy's eyes. That had been a really good joke on Jimmy, Hogue thought, even though no one else seemed particularly amused by it.

The cook was one of those men who do not much care what anyone else says or does, but some of the regular hands had begun drifting in to the evening fire ready for their supper and were standing around smoking and watching after a full day in the saddle.

One of them—Hogue could no longer remember who it might have been—gave Hogue a sharp glance that should have been a warning and went to the cook's wagon for a pot of grease drippings that was always kept available there for purposes of frying meat or greasing the wagon axles or softening leather or whatever else might be required.

The man carried the pot to the kid and used a wooden spoon to sling a dollop of the salty grease into Jimmy's palm. He gave Hogue another sharp look but did not say anything to him.

Hogue shrugged it off and made sure he was the first one in line when it came time for the meal to be served up. He ate quickly, as had become his habit, primarily because all of the hands ate quickly, and dragged his saddle out of the bed wagon, ready for his night's work.

That saddle was not much to look at and had been available at a bargain price because the tree was cracked, but Hogue was proud of it. He bought it, wrapped the tree with green rawhide and sat it with pride. This year, by damn, it was *his* saddle he was sitting, not some borrowed thing, and therefore it was as fine as any hand-carved, concha-mounted, custom-made article you could buy in San Antonio, and everyone knew that the best saddles anywhere were the ones that were made in San Antonio.

He looped his bridle over his shoulder and carried his gear out to where the remuda was being held inside a rope corral while the men came in to offsaddle their day's choice of mounts and catch out their night horses. The night horses would be kept on picket ropes close to camp while Hogue herded the rest of the remuda anywhere they could find good grass and not be too close to the bunched and rested herd of cattle.

Hogue dropped his saddle onto the ground and took his rope from its keeper beside the horn. He was not much good with a rope. Not yet. That would not come until much practice and a fair number of years had passed. But he was competent enough to catch the horse he wanted, given a small enough area to work in and a good many tries in which to do the catching. He slipped under the stake-held corral rope and carried his rope and bridle into the flimsy enclosure with the waiting horses.

He knew the one he wanted, which was a bald-faced spotted horse that no one else wanted because of the white on its feet and lower legs. Everyone knew that white feet were soft and likely to go lame no matter how carefully a man did his shoeing. Still, Hogue liked the horse because it had a remarkably smooth, indeed lazy way of going that made it easy for the rider to catch a little sleep while he was nighthawking.

The horse did not particularly want to be caught this evening and kept ducking away from Hogue's sloppy loops. Hogue did not yet know enough to build a small loop and throw it straight and fast, nor how to roll a loop under the neck of another horse to forefoot the one he wanted. He kept trying to catch his animal with large loops and a great deal of arm motion, and that simply was not working. After half a dozen tries he became angry with the horse—not himself, certainly—and turned around in disgust to cool off for a moment before he made another try.

It was getting on toward dark now and the light was poor, but even so he could see that some damned rodent, a weasel or a marten or some such fool thing, was nosing around at Hogue's saddle, probably attracted there by the salt of horse sweat or perhaps by the grease that was used to soften and preserve leather as old and worn as that in Hogue's fourth- or fifth-hand saddle.

Whatever had brought the little animal out, Hogue did not want it chewing on any part of that fine saddle. And he was not going to stand for it.

Without thinking, Hogue yanked out the decrepit old hawg-laig from his belt and threw down on the intruder.

There was only one chance in three that the gun would fire anyway, but this time it did.

More than that, the burning powder from that chamber ignited an adjacent chamber's powder charge, and there was one hell of a bang when the gun went off.

The pistol twisted sideways and threw Hogue's arm high. At the same time, the twin charges of explosive powder created a fireball in the dusk that seemed four times as great as the already huge gouts of flame that came from a normal discharge of a cap-and-ball revolver.

Hogue let out a yelp of surprise and let go of the offending weapon, which flew high into the air, as his arm was already moving in that direction.

Noise, flame and flying objects—all together they were just too much for the remuda, which was already more than a little nervous from all the commotion Hogue had been causing in their midst with his unfancy rope work.

The horses dropped their heads and laid their ears back, gave one loud collective snort of alarm and fled.

One strand of hemp rope was not going to stop them. In all probability a four-rail fence would not have stopped them.

The horses snorted and stamped and were gone, leaving Hogue in the center of a fallen rope with his hands empty and a rather foolish expression on his face.

He looked around, but the horses were no longer anywhere in sight.

When he looked back, at least half of the crew were standing there looking at him.

"Go fetch 'em in, boy," one of the men said.

"I don't have—" He had been about to say that he did not have a horse to ride after them. But that was rather obvious already. Hogue shut up and swallowed back the words, hitched his bridle higher onto his shoulder and began walking.

It was well past dawn before he got back to camp.

At least he had been able to recover all of the horses. One of them must have fallen, because it had a large, swollen lump on its near shoulder, but at least he did have all of them back.

At that, though, the day's work had been delayed, and if any of the men had any really hard riding to do that day they might find themselves on horses that would not be as fresh as they should have been. Hogue was in trouble and he knew it.

No one said a word to him, though, when he brought the

remuda back into the rope enclosure, which had been re-erected in his absence. No one spoke to him while he slipped as quietly and as unobtrusively as he could to the fire and helped himself to a tin plate of breakfast. Everyone sat in complete silence while he ate. Or tried to. He finally gave up trying to swallow the sawdust-dry bites of whatever it was he was having and set his plate aside.

"Hog, we got to thank you," one of the men said.

"Yessir?" Hogue was feeling more than a bit subdued and was not inclined toward smart-alec remarks at that moment.

"Yes, we do, Hog. Fact is, we haven't had much to talk about here lately. Just the usual old stuff. Now we're gonna have somethin' new to discuss, other than which steer's got the widest horns."

"What d'you . . . ?"

He grinned. "Why, Hog, ol' son, we're gonna have us a trial. An' *you* are the guest of honor."

Oh, they had had a trial, all right.

One of the crew, the one who had helped Jimmy the hey-boy the evening before, acted as the prosecutor. Everyone else acted as jury. There was no defense counsel because, as a member of the jury cheerfully explained, "Yer guiltier'n hell anyhow, so there ain't no reason fer one."

The prosecutor was able to come up with an impressively long list of Hogue's assorted sins, commenting on this one, acting that one out with a theretofore undisplayed gift of mimicry and mime.

The man had Hogue's swagger and tone of voice down pat, and he used both to great effect.

Before he was done, he had the entire jury, including young Jimmy, in tears with howling laughter.

Before he was done he even had *Hogue* going into fits of laughter. Which probably helped make the experience less painful than it might otherwise have been.

When they were done, which was not until lunchtime, the jury was polled and the men one by one solemnly declared that Hog Bynell was, as the man had said, "guiltier'n hell."

Hogue marched himself willingly to the nearest wheel of the cook wagon, shucked his britches on command and bent himself over the iron rim while one of the men removed his chaps and soaked them in the water barrel. The wet leather was then applied with some vigor to Hogue's backside, including several good swings that were offered by Jimmy the hey-boy.

It hurt, all right, but not really all that much. It might have hurt a great deal worse if the men had not all been laughing when they swung. But by this time the object lesson had turned into an entertainment form much more than a form of punishment, and none of the blows were delivered with malice. Not even those applied by Jimmy. Hogue grinned at them when they were done.

He also accepted the experience as a lesson of sorts. There was a distinct difference between pride and arrogance. The first was considered to be more than acceptable on the trail; the latter would not long be tolerated.

After that, Hogue got along quite well for the remainder of that drive. And for a good many afterward.

Come to think of it, he reflected now, he did not know what had happened to that old pistol. He did not remember ever seeing it again after that chain fire.

He chuckled and thought about how his bottom had smarted when it hit the saddle *that* night. Whew!

CHAPTER 25

There was still a trace of smile on Hogue's lips when he turned his head to see what the noise was that Trapp had just made behind him. The man was sucking at a bottle again. The sight of the hint of smile seemed to infuriate him as soon as he saw it.

"What are you looking at, cripple? Huh? Huh?" Al stepped forward and punctuated each "huh" with a hard blow to the side of Hogue's head.

Hogue shrugged and turned his head away. He ignored the punches, genuinely not caring about them. Any slight amount of pain that Al Trapp might cause him now would be only temporary in any event.

It was odd, Hogue thought, how a man's perspective could change like that. He had tried not to care about pain before; now he really did not care. Al could punch and pummel all he wanted. It would not bother Hogue. Not in the long run.

In a way his decision had freed Hogue. He felt very much at peace and not at all concerned about what Trapp or Chuck or anyone else might do. That was nice, Hogue thought.

Sometime during his chain of thought, Trapp quit hitting him. That was all right too.

Actually, Hogue thought, there was no reason at all why he should not try to do something constructive with his last few hours.

In fact, if some constructive act were to turn out to be his last act, why, that would be rather nice. Yes it would, Hogue decided. Rather nice.

An act like, say, stopping the robbers from halting that train. Not that the money mattered. But Hogue would like to know that the crews of those two trains did not have to die because of Hogue Bynell's worthlessness. That would be a very nice thing to be able to remember. Assuming that memory would be possible. Hogue was very unclear about what was supposed to happen to a person after death. There was uncertainty enough about life without going into all the extra complications posed by thinking about death and what might come afterward. It was not a subject Hogue had given much thought to. In any event it would be nice to know for as long as was possible that he had not killed any trainmen.

The ghost of a smile forgotten but still clinging to his lips, Hogue reached for his crutches and levered himself upright.

"Where the hell do you think . . . ?"

Hogue did not hear Al's question. He stood and with deliberate calm tucked the padded crosspiece of one crutch under his left arm to give him balance. The other he inverted and held with both hands.

"I *asked* you. . . ."

Hogue swung the crutch. He had seen a little boy swing a stick at a hard, white ball once. He did not know the name of the game that was being played, but he had admired the economy of motion and the apparent power that went into the boy's swing. Now he swung his crutch in much the same manner.

Too late, Al realized that something had gone seriously

amiss with their apparently cowed cripple. Trapp jerked an arm up over his face in an effort to fend off the blow.

The slim, heavy double billet of wood whistled through the air in a swift arc that ended when the hickory shaft smashed into the side of Al Trapp's face, splintering his cheekbone and breaking his jaw with a snap that was as loud as the crunch of breaking wood had been. Trapp went down like a poleaxed shoat.

Hogue was unclear about the sequence of events over the next few seconds.

There was the sound of boot steps and a great deal of shouting. He knew that for a fact.

One of the others—Hogue had a vague impression that it was J. Kenneth Harlinton, improbable though that seemed—picked Hogue up and slammed him back against the edge of the big desk, almost breaking Hogue's back in the process.

The other one, it might have been Chuck, was bent over Al Trapp's fallen form.

There was more shouting, some cries of anger and possibly even of fright. Hogue was still carrying what was left of his broken crutch. The fragment of wood was torn away from him.

Hogue expected to be beaten with his own club. He did not particularly care that he would be, but he did expect it. Instead both Chuck and J. Kenneth now were bent over Trapp.

Hogue was surprised to find himself on the floor too now. He did not remember falling after he hit the desk. He pulled the chair closer and began to climb up it until he could swing around and drop into place on the seat. The horsehair-covered cushion on the seat had long since formed itself to

Hogue's body shape. It felt comforting now as well as comfortable.

Trapp was not moving, had not moved since he hit the floor without so much as a bounce. There was a little blood on the floor beside his head. Not much, just more than a trace of it.

Chuck looked up at Hogue dispassionately. "You killed him surer'n hell," he said calmly.

Hogue felt curious rather than frightened now. He fully expected Chuck to retaliate for the death of his partner, either to use his revolver to blow Hogue's brains out or to batter him to death with the piece of crutch that was now lying on the floor between them. Hogue would have preferred the gun but did not really care all that much either way.

"You're sure about that?" he asked.

"I said I was. Broke his head." Chuck prodded the side of his ex-partner's skull. "Feels like mush."

"I don't guess I will apologize," Hogue said.

Chuck grunted. He was looking at Hogue with a cold calculation that it took no great talent to be able to read as impending murder.

"I wouldn't." Hogue had almost forgotten about the little rummy who was kneeling on the floor beside Chuck, but it was J. Kenneth who had spoken. He laid a hand lightly on Chuck's forearm, not to restrain him but to underline his words. "You and Al were never that close, Charles. Certainly not close enough to jeopardize the success of this, um, venture of yours. You still might need Mr. Bynell there."

"He did kill Al."

"Yes, and if necessary you can dispose of him. *After* the westbound has passed through and you know that everything is proceeding as it should." The little man's voice was still mellow and cultured.

Hogue was more than a bit surprised, but it seemed that neither of them regarded the loss of Al Trapp as being extremely serious.

"It's a matter of principle," Chuck said.

"Fine," J. Kenneth agreed. "But do wait until later. You never know what might happen. As witness our friend here. Would you have thought he would be able to kill Alonzo? Certainly I never would have entertained that as a possibility. I doubt that you would either. So do wait, Charles. You might still need him."

Chuck grunted and said, "We already have the paper we needed."

"You do indeed, but I do not have Mr. Bynell's hand on the key. There is yet a few minutes to wait, Charles. Do you want to take the risk? Or face the consequences if you guess wrongly? I think not."

"Where is the damn paper anyhow? We don't want him tearin' it up the way he tore ol' Al's head up."

J. Kenneth patted his breast pocket. "I have it right here."

"Put it in the pouch. Go ahead an' do it now, and do it right. And don't let him"—he jerked a thumb toward Hogue —"near it. You don't need him for that."

"Whatever you say, Charles."

J. Kenneth got to his feet slowly. He moved with the deliberate control of a physically feeble person, and Hogue wondered how the little man could have had enough strength to fling him aside the way J. Kenneth seemed to have done a few minutes before.

"I suggest," J. Kenneth said, "that we take the precaution of removing this second crutch from Mr. Bynell's reach also."

"I'll do it." Chuck left his dead partner's side and picked up the crutch from where it had fallen. He stood and towered over the seated figure before him. Looking Hogue square in the eye, obviously wishing that he was about to strike Hogue's head instead of the unfeeling wood of the desk, Chuck threw the single remaining crutch out the door. "Now try an' go someplace," he said in a voice that contained a threat despite its softness of tone.

Hogue shrugged. Now or later, gun or club, it really did not much matter. He turned his head and looked at the body on the floor between his desk and his bunk. Al looked smaller now than he had when he was alive.

CHAPTER 26

Hogue Bynell had never killed a man before. Not in all those years and all those brawls. Never.

Oh, there had been opportunities enough, he supposed. There had never before been a necessity for it. Perhaps there had not been a necessity to kill now. Certainly there had not been a necessity to kill now, Hogue decided. Hogue was going to die anyway. It hardly mattered whether he did it himself or allowed Al Trapp to do it for him. So there had been no necessity to kill this time either. Now that he thought about it, it was plain enough. A minute or so before, he had not had time to do that kind of thinking or Al Trapp would still be alive.

Instead he was a deflated shell of what had been a man, an empty husk with the ear of corn ripped away and the husk discarded.

Hogue looked at him and shivered.

Always before, fighting had been something he did in fun or, once in a while, in a spurt of hot anger. Never coldly. Never with indifference.

Maybe, he thought, that was the difference between a good old boy and a killer. A good old boy fought, sure, but it was a form of entertainment and a release. A killer must fight coldly. Hogue had always thought of himself as a good old boy, a hand. But that was the way things used to be. Now he did not know.

He thought back, trying to remember the few times in the past when he had seen men who were killers. Or who were said to be killers.

There were few enough of those times. Very few indeed, considering all the places he had been and the things he had done with his life.

Hogue had never personally seen any of those men who were legendary in their reputations as killers. He had heard about them. He had listened to stories about them and songs that were made up about them. But he had never seen any of them. Not in Newton or Ellsworth or Dodge City or Tascosa or Cheyenne. The closest he had ever come to seeing any of those legendary killers had been a few holes in a few walls where someone would point to them and say that So-and-so had put that hole there when he gunned down thus-and-such other fellow. But, hell, no one ever believed that kind of bull, including the man who was telling the story. It was just a way to get a visitor to stand a round of drinks. Everyone knew that, including the man who was being taken for the price of the round.

The closest Hogue had ever come to seeing a real killer, he thought, was once in Fort Griffin when a seedy-looking kid in a shapeless coat and needing a haircut was pointed out to him as Will Young. Hogue had never heard of anybody named Will Young, but the local man said Young was pure hell with a gun and had shot he did not know how many men. Seven or eight at the very least.

Hogue remembered that he had not been impressed much. Young had looked like just another down-at-the-heels yahoo, as far as he could see, the only difference between him and anyone else being that he was all alone at one end of the bar where they had been and was not talking to anyone, including the bartender. Nothing special about him except that he was being ignored by everyone around him and was ignoring them back.

There had been that time, Hogue remembered, and then there was the hanging Hogue had gone to once down in Big Spring.

There had been no question that that fellow had been a murderer. Tried and convicted for it. There had been a dispute over a milk cow, and this man—Hogue could no longer remember his name—had cut down on the offending neighbor and blew a milk-pail-sized hole in the man's liver with a scatter-gun. Wounded a couple of others, too.

The convict never said a word on the scaffold, Hogue remembered. Never seemed to take much interest at all in what was going on around him. All of the excitement that time had been in the crowd, with families coming in from all around the country, bringing the kids and packing baskets of lunch and buying souvenirs from the vendors who had showed up to hawk jewelry and medicines and imitation-silk neckerchiefs with the date embroidered in one corner. The excitement had all been in the crowd, not in the man who was being hanged. The fellow had not even kicked much when he dropped. And the smelly mess that had come afterward, well, that could not be blamed on a man who was already dead.

No, Hogue thought, both of those two examples had seemed darn well aloof from the rest of the world.

Not at all the way Hogue had felt that one time he thought he might have killed someone.

, That had been in Canada, in the Panhandle country, in a barroom fight that threatened to get serious when the fellow Hogue was fighting with pulled a knife and took a slash at Hogue's gut.

His name—Hogue had not known it at the time but he had sure found out about it afterward—was Cooper. George Tomlinson Cooper. They called him Tommy or sometimes Coop.

He had pulled the knife and made his cut and did manage to slice some buttons and the front of Hogue's vest, and it turned out to be a fortunate thing that he was wearing a leather vest that did not cut so handily as cloth would have.

Hogue had gotten mad then. Really mad, not like in a normal fight when mad was just an excuse to have the fight, and he had set in to kicking Tommy Cooper. In the cods to drop him and then in the ribs and belly and the side of his head. He had hardly known what he was doing, he was so mad, and some of Cooper's friends had finally pulled him off the unconscious cowboy and held onto Hogue until he got his senses back.

They thought at first that Cooper was dead and then they decided that he was dying, and Hogue could still remember the sick feeling in his own gut when he looked down at Tommy Cooper on that floor and thought that maybe he had killed the man.

Hogue had helped them carry Cooper to a room and sat there while a doctor was brought to bind and bandage him and mix some powders to pour into him, and Hogue had sat in that room helping with the nursemaiding for the better part of three days before they were all satisfied that Cooper would get better. Hogue had paid every penny of the doctor's fee and the room rent and would have signed away his hope for Salvation, too, just to know that Tommy Cooper was going to get well again.

It had been a sick, empty, terrible feeling that time, and relief had been more potent than a jug of Taos whiskey the first time Tommy Cooper opened his eyes and looked like he could know what he was seeing.

That had been some time, Hogue thought.

Now. . . .

He looked around behind him.

There was no doctor who was going to mix a powder and make Al Trapp open his eyes and see again.

The difference was that this time Hogue did not care.

That was odd, he thought.

He really *ought* to care. He had taken a human life. He ought to care about that. At least a little. He did not.

Hogue searched inside himself, wondering about that, trying to examine why he felt so detached from the whole thing. That did not seem right, somehow.

He looked again at Al Trapp's cooling body.

No, he decided, there was nothing that he—

Hogue jerked his swivel chair sharply to the side and began to vomit onto the plank floor of the railroad shack.

CHAPTER 27

Hogue did not want to feel anything, care about anything. It seemed rather obscene to be feeling emotions and caring about having taken a life now that he was as good as a dead man himself. Particularly since it was his own idea that he should be a dead man.

Make Chuck Porter do it for him or do it himself—what should that matter? It should not matter. Somehow Hogue could not quite make himself believe that it did not matter.

And it was funny, he thought, that he was no longer fretting about the reason he had come to that decision.

Useless. Utterly without value. That was the reason for it all. Worthless old one-legged Hogue Bynell. Hogue knew he was worthless. So had Al Trapp. But now Trapp was dead, and it was worthless, useless, valueless old Hogue who had killed him. And Trapp's friends had not even bothered—not yet—to avenge their partner. Hogue still sat in the shack with them, waiting for the westbound to go through and pick up the message pouch so a bunch of other thugs and cretins could help themselves to a payroll. While their buddy Al lay dead on the floor of Relay 12.

Wouldn't that make Trapp angry? Hogue thought. Furious, he agreed with himself. It really would. Just being killed by a worthless cripple would be enough to make him furious. The rest of it would be piling insult onto fatal injury.

Hogue shook his head. Having thoughts like those, he wondered if he might be going crazy in addition to everything else. He wrinkled his nose. The smell of his vomit was sharply sour and unpleasant. He would have gone outside if he could, but one crutch was broken, smashed to splinters against Al Trapp's skull, and the other one had been taken away from him. Hogue was not expected to need crutches ever again, though. Chuck expected to see to that.

Hogue sighed. Off on the other side of the shack, Chuck and J. Kenneth were discussing him, Chuck speculating out loud that they really did not need Hogue any longer, so they really should go ahead and put him out of their way, J. Kenneth advising caution just to be sure. Hogue pulled his railroad-issue watch from his pocket. Had he wound it that morning? He could not remember now. He wound it—carefully, lightly so as to make sure he did not overwind it and jam the sensitive spring mechanism—just to make sure. It was still running, at any rate. There was very little time left before the westbound would come rumbling through, picking up the message pouch on the way past and shaking the small shack with the immense power of its drivers when it roared by without a pause.

There would be a pause soon enough, Hogue knew. There would be a pause at the siding long enough for a bunch of shouting, shooting idiots to come tumbling out of those rocks and grab off the payroll.

That would be nothing to the pause that would take place afterward.

The delay would be more than enough to ensure that the westbound payroll train would run smack into the engine of the eastbound special that would be riding the single set of rails straight for them.

That pause would be a permanent thing for the engine crews on both trains, maybe for their brakemen as well.

How many men? Hogue wondered. How many would die there? Would they bury them there at the accident scene? No, he did not think so.

Someone would come along with sledgehammers and spikes to replace the rails that would be torn up and with hoists and winches to right the rolling stock and lift it back onto the tracks and with wooden boxes to hold the bodies of the men who were dead. A good many wooden boxes, if Hogue was any judge of it. They would take the boxes with them, to wherever the men had been from, and there would be families to gather around and cry and friends to tell lies about how fine each of the dead men had been. Hogue wondered what friends would gather and what lies they would tell over the box that would be hauled away from Relay 12.

None, he thought bitterly.

No, dammit, he told himself sternly. It was a lousy time for lying, even to himself.

There would be the boys from the Y Knot. There would be Mabel Cutcheon. She was a good woman, and they had been something to each other once, might have been even more if he had not been so sensitive about things that she swore bothered him more than they would ever disturb her, and so she would come. Out of a sense of duty if nothing else. And the boys from the Y Knot. They were a good crew. They came around to see him when he was alive, in spite of the way he treated them. If they were friends good enough to stand for Hogue's sourness when he was alive, they would damn sure be good enough friends to come and lie over his coffin when he was dead.

Even some of the men from the line might come. Maybe the crew from the work train or some of the men from the terminus office. Hogue wished briefly that he had made some carvings for those men's children, the way they had wanted him to. It was too late to do anything about it now, of course, but if he had it to do over again he would do it differently.

He thought with more than a twinge of regret that he might have brought some real joy into some of those families back wherever the train crewmen lived. He could carve a fine animal; he probably could carve one hell of a doll if he ever set his mind to it. He just bet that he could have done that. He wondered whose homes he would be sending pine coffins into instead of the carved figures and cute dolls he really should have made but did not.

He wondered briefly what would happen to the pay he still had on account on the company books. He had no idea how much it was, but it should be a fair amount by now. For sure he hardly ever used any of it.

He could leave it to someone, he thought. Mabel Cutcheon or maybe some of the children of the men who would die in the wreck when those two trains collided. That was probably the better idea, he thought, but how do you word a will for the money to go to the issue of someone who is not dead yet? Because probably the wreck would happen after Hogue was already dead. He would not be able to know who or how many or hardly anything at all that a man should know when he sits down to write out his will. He wondered if it would even be possible to word it out, even if he were a lawyer, which of course he was not. He shook his head. There were as many complications to dying, it seemed, as there were to living.

Hogue sighed. It was such a shame there was no longer time for him to make a carving or . . . *something*. He wished he would be able to leave *something* behind. Almost anything. Anything except a memory that he was the one who caused a head-on and took those lives. Because that was sure to happen. That was a lousy legacy for a man to leave behind, even a useless, one-legged man.

But that was damn sure all Hogue Bynell would be leaving behind him. That was a thought more bitter than any of the others Hogue had been having this day. And that was all he would be leaving. No kids, not even a horse and saddle to be delivered over to some chosen friend.

He looked around behind him, toward his bunk. There was certainly nothing of any value over there to be distributed. Nothing that anyone in his right mind would want. The food and liquor would be used up by the next Relay 12 operator. Unless that fellow turned out to be a tall, underweight, one-legged son of a bitch, the clothing would all be burned. The letters would mean nothing to anyone. The carvings had all gone into the firebox. There was nothing else. Nothing at all left from the life he had led. And when he was gone there would not even be memories of it. Except that one last one, everyone remembering that a man named Hogue Bynell had been the one to cause the big wreck that killed however many men it turned out to be and orphaned however many children who would grow up despising his name.

That was some damned legacy, all right, Hogue thought.

He was getting maudlin again. He knew that. He wished he also knew how to stop it.

He looked up. Chuck Porter had his revolver out and was idly toying with it in his hands. *That* would stop it, all right.

Hogue felt a wave of resentment sweep through him.

You have no right to do this to me, he wanted to shout at Charles Porter. *You have no right.*

CHAPTER 28

Hogue glared at Porter, his resentment growing and threatening to overwhelm him.

Chuck saw the expression and before he could realize what he was doing recoiled from it. He jerked and half turned in his chair, as if about to run, before he seemed to realize what he was doing and regained control of himself.

"You damned worthless cripple," he snapped. The revolver in his hand steadied on Hogue's chest, and for a moment Hogue thought Chuck was going to pull the trigger then and there and not wait until the train had passed.

"That's right," Hogue agreed. "Worthless. I must be. I did what you bastards wanted me to. But not so worthless that your buddy ain't lying there dead on the floor."

"I'm not forgetting that either, cripple. When we're done with you, you'll answer for killing Al. Just see if you don't."

Hogue laughed. He was genuinely unafraid of Porter now. Hell, there was nothing left for him to be afraid of. Not any longer. "I can wait," he said lightly.

"Keep acting like you were a minute ago an' you won't have to wait any more," Chuck threatened.

Hogue smiled at him. "Afraid, Chuck? Of a worthless, one-legged man? And you with a gun in your hand? Now, that ought to kinda tickle me. It's a compliment, in a way. I think it does tickle me, in fact. Yeah, I'm sure of it."

"Shut up." Porter looked away from him.

"Whatever you say, Charles. After all, you have the gun."

"Don't you forget it neither."

"I won't. That's a promise."

Hogue was feeling better. In fact he was feeling pretty good. He looked at J. Kenneth and gave the little telegrapher a wink. J. Kenneth looked away from him too. What J. Kenneth was telegraphing now was nervousness.

By damn, Hogue thought, both of these fellows were getting nervous around him now. He had killed Al Trapp, who was supposed to be the mean one of this crowd, and now both of the others were acting like they were half scared of him. More than half, maybe. For sure they were uneasy. Even if Hogue did have only the one leg and a reputation for uselessness.

Or maybe, to give himself the small scrap that was his due, maybe his reputation was not actually for being so useless at that.

He had, after all, been a helluva hand when he still had both his legs.

And since then he had been a better-than-fair telegraph operator.

That was the truth, too. The whole section of the line knew that if Hogue Bynell sent it, it was right. If he posted an order, it was correct and would be obeyed. No matter how strange it might sound, it had to be right, because Hogue Bynell just did not make mistakes. If that was because he was so uninterested in anything outside his lousy little relay shack that he was never distracted from his job, well, so what? The fact remained, he was the most reliable damned operator on the section. That was probably a large part of the reason Porter and J. Kenneth and the dead Al Trapp were here right now. With some other operator, an engineer might well have questioned an order that put a large payroll car onto a siding out in the middle of the big lonesome. But if the order came from Relay 12 it had to be accurate. Right?

Damn straight, Hogue told himself.

And now these miserable outlaws were beginning to be afraid of him.

So maybe ol' Hogue had been doing some underestimating around here, he told himself. If a rough customer like Porter could be afraid of him or a cultured, educated man—and deadbeat rummy or no, J. Kenneth was both of those—could be worried about him, it was just possible that they might have reason to be.

For that matter, Mabel Cutcheon was a fine woman. Not the sort to go silly over nothing at all. That was one of the things that Hogue admired about her. And she had always claimed to find enough to favor about him, before the accident but afterward, too.

And the little bits of nothing that were inside the Relay 12 shack were almighty little for a man to leave behind him. There ought to be more than that to show for a man's life.

Maybe . . . maybe there could be. If he set his mind to it. If he decided to get his back up and *do* something instead of waiting for the end like some sulled-up old cow that has called it quits and lies down to wait to die. Hogue never could understand that before in man or animal, although he had seen it happen in both. Now he had been doing it himself. *Had* been. He did not have to if he did not want to. Not any more he did not.

Hogue looked across the room at Chuck Porter and at the gun in the outlaw's hand. There was a look of quiet speculation in Hogue's gaze.

CHAPTER 29

"I got to go to the backhouse."

"What?"

"I said—"

"I heard that part, dammit," Chuck snapped. "Can't you hold it?"

"I've been holding it. Now I got to go. But I got to have my crutch to do it with." Hogue gave the blocky man a look of mingled disgust and exasperation. "Man, I ain't gonna run off nowhere. An' you got the gun. Your damn pouch is hanging out there on the hook ready for pickup. What am I gonna do, leap up that pole an' snatch it down without you seeing? Come off it. I just gotta go, that's all. Hell, I didn't *plan* it."

Porter looked annoyed. He also looked nervous. About Hogue probably but also almost certainly about the train that was due to arrive within minutes. He glanced at his watch and then at J. Kenneth.

J. Kenneth shrugged and looked away.

"You can hold it a few minutes more."

"I can't, I tell you."

Hogue looked angry. He rose from his chair and tried to hop forward on his one leg, but the leg seemed to buckle for a moment. He had taken quite a beating earlier and could have been none too strong now. He toppled and flailed his arms.

Hogue grabbed at the back of his chair but its casters let it roll aside. He made another desperate grab for the iron-hinged wooden lever that stood beside his desk, but that just moved on its hinge and gave way beneath him.

He fell heavily to the floor and lay in a sprawl near Al Trapp's body. As he lay there, a dark, wet stain spread across the front of his trousers.

Porter and now even J. Kenneth Harlinton broke into loud laughter as a look of acute embarrassment spread across Hogue's face.

Hogue turned his head away. Muttering softly to himself, he began the painfully slow and difficult process of pulling himself back upright and into his chair. He sat staring stonily toward the blank wall of the shack near the doorway.

CHAPTER 30

They could hear the high-pitched, moaning screech of the train whistle.

Porter closed the cover on his watch and tucked it away in a pocket. "Right on the money." He guffawed. "Right on a whole bunch of money, get it?" He and J. Kenneth were both smiling now.

Hogue, pretending to ignore them, was holding his breath.

The train order, written in Hogue's own hand and following the exact style specified by the line, was hanging in its pouch on the hook outside. As soon as the engineer read that order, he was as good as a dead man. If the outlaws did not kill him, and probably they would not, then the eastbound special would. But, either way, he was a dead man and so would be any who were riding in the engine with him.

The train was coming closer now. They could hear the clatter of steel on steel as the wheels hit rail joints and were jolted on their axles, the hard steel of the wheels banging on the hard steel of the rails.

A moment more and they could hear the powerful, muted roar of the driving engine as well.

It would just be so much noise to Porter and to J. Kenneth. To Hogue there was a particular quality in the sound that brought a smile to his lips and a leap of fierce pleasure to his heart.

Hogue swiveled his chair to face Charles Porter. He felt perfectly safe in doing so. He doubted that at this moment either of the other men remembered his existence.

In another few moments they would again be aware of him. But not now.

CHAPTER 31

"Aren't they going rather slowly for a flying pickup?" J. Kenneth asked. There was a hint of beginning alarm in his voice.

"They can't be, they're—Gawda'mighty, they're stopping!!!" Porter stood with his revolver clutched in his hand and stared incredulously out the open door toward the track, a matter of only feet away.

The engine had already passed the platform, but there could be no doubt now that the following cars were moving very slowly indeed or that what speed they did have continued to diminish.

The men inside the shack could hear the sharp, whining squeal of set brakes protesting against their load and now the shouts of brakemen who rode atop the boxcars.

Porter took a step forward, as if to move in wonder for the doorway. Or perhaps to bolt toward it.

His concentration was on what was happening outside the shack, and he may not even have seen the tall, angry form that was leaping across the small room toward him with a curious, hopping motion.

With the agility of long practice, Hogue was bounding across the room, his one leg driving him with a speed that very nearly approached that of a two-legged man.

One rope-hardened hand clamped down on the wrist of

Chuck's gun hand, and the other attached itself firmly to the outlaw's throat.

J. Kenneth threw himself aside in a sudden panic, but for the moment he had been forgotten by friend and foe alike.

Hogue threw himself onto Porter, and his weight carried both of them to the floor, slamming into the still warm side of the stove and dropping down to the planking, where Porter's physical advantage was lessened if not completely eliminated.

Hogue no longer cared about advantages or disadvantages anyway. He had Porter's wrist in one hand and throat in another, and this was very nearly the old sort of rough-and-tumble Hogue had found himself in so many times before. Punch if you can. Claw, scratch, bite and kick; do whatever it takes to win. Hogue did.

Porter had been there too, and he was a powerful man.

The outlaw ignored the grip on his gun hand, ignored for the moment the much more dangerous grasp around his throat and tried to knee Hogue in the crotch.

The maneuver was expected. Hogue blocked the knee with his thigh and found the needed motion was even easier with no leg beneath that thigh to get tangled up in his opponent's legs. He laughed into Charles Porter's ear and followed that by sinking his teeth into the same ear.

The two of them rolled over and over, crashing into the stove again and knocking it askew with a billow of black soot that rained down onto both of them.

Porter was raining punches onto Hogue's neck and shoulders with his free hand. He succeeded in knocking Hogue's hand away from his throat. Hogue shifted the point of his attack and began punching Porter in the belly as, still tangled, they rolled over and over.

A leg of Hogue's bunk collapsed as the two bodies jammed into it, and the side of the bunk fell, catching Hogue painfully across the top of the head.

Blood from a cut flooded Hogue's eyes. He released his bite on Porter's ear long enough to bury his face against the other man's shoulder and wipe the blood out of his eyes with Porter's shirt. Then he levered himself higher against Porter's body and again clamped his teeth into the bleeding ear. Porter screamed and began to pummel Hogue all the harder.

J. Kenneth was backed into a corner now, looking like a cornered and very frightened rabbit.

"Help me, you little bastard," Porter shouted at him. "Grab a club. Anything. *Do* something."

J. Kenneth's eyes darted outside the relay shack toward the track. The train was at a full stop now.

J. Kenneth did something. If not exactly what he had been ordered, he at least did do something. He picked himself up and stretched his legs, making a dash for the open doorway and the freedom of the big-grass country beyond it.

Porter saw him go. He opened his mouth and might have shouted something at his departing partner except that at that moment the growing numbness caused by Hogue's grip on his wrist made him lose his hold on the revolver, and the gun fell to the floor between the two men.

Both grabbed for it, but Hogue was the quicker, if only because Porter had so little sense of feeling left in that hand. Hogue grabbed the gun by the barrel and began trying to bash the butt into Porter's skull.

It was no longer a fight at that point. Porter was no longer interested in doing any damage to Hogue, he was intent on trying to keep Hogue from caving his skull in the way Al

Trapp's had turned to a dead, mush-soft pocket where Hogue had hit him.

The two men were still on the floor locked in that combat when the MK&C engineer and his fireman stalked into the relay station to ask the operator just what in the hell was going on around there.

CHAPTER 32

A pair of brakemen, burly and hardened by their work, by exposure to the elements and by the even harder life they lived when their working hours were over, came stomping into the tiny shack. They dragged a shrunken-looking, terrified J. Kenneth Harlinton between them.

"This would be the other'n?" one of them asked.

Hogue smiled. "It would for a fact, boys. Welcome back, J. Kenneth."

"You will explain to them, I hope, that I did try to help you, that I did make every attempt to—"

"I'll tell 'em you tried to help hold up the train," Hogue said, cutting the little man short. He grinned. "You might find this kinda hard to understand, J. Kenneth. An' ol' Chuck here too. But railroaders get real irritated when somebody tries to cause a head-on. *Real* upset."

Still grinning, he looked Chuck's way, and J. Kenneth followed the motion of Hogue's eyes.

What J. Kenneth saw there was hardly encouraging. Porter had been in a tussle when J. Kenneth left so hurriedly, but the man had not been in bad shape. Now his face looked much like a mask hastily fashioned from ground meat.

"We could use a little information from you, J. Kenneth. You know. Stuff like how many fellas are waiting up there for the train to pull in at the siding. How they're armed.

How they figure to approach the train. Stuff like that. Unless, of course, you want your new pals there to talk to you like these other railroadin' boys have been talkin' to Chuck." Hogue grinned. "It's your choice."

J. Kenneth swallowed very hard. "But what . . . ?"

"What happened? Is that what you're asking?" Hogue laughed and so did a half dozen of the railroad men and baggage-car guards who were crowded into the little shack.

"Well, I'll tell you what happened, J. Kenneth. You know that red-ball flag out on the post? No? Take my word for it, it's there. Never been used before, but it's there. Standard-issue stuff. The railroad puts one on every platform, right along with the hook for the pouch you boys were so bent on hanging out there.

"Like I say, it's never been used before, but it's there. What it is, you see, is a signal to stop the train. For freight or passengers or whatever.

"You boys hung the pouch all right, an' that was picked up with the hook just like you intended. But a little while ago when you and Chuck was laughing so hard about the crip fallin' down and wetting himself, well, that lever I fell down against is what throws the signal.

"Jake here," he hooked a thumb toward the engineer in his floppy, striped cap, "thought it was odd as hell to see a pouch and a red ball too, but rules are rules, and he went by the book. Hooked in the pouch an' stopped the train at the signal."

Hogue was grinning. J. Kenneth was not. Jake was grinning. Charles Porter, at his feet, was unconscious.

"Now, J. Kenneth, if you'd be kind enough to tell us what we want to know. . . ."

J. Kenneth complied, eagerly if not happily, answering

every question the railroad men put to him and offering more tidbits of information that they did not think to ask.

"I'll be riding along with you," Hogue said much later.

"I don't think—" the straw boss of the guard detail began to say, but the engineer cut him off.

"Shut up, Lou. If Bynell says he's going, then he's going. He's earned the right."

"But he only has. . . ."

"One leg? Damn straight he only has one leg. So what? A man don't need any legs to shoot a rifle or to be smart enough to think straight. Hell, he thought straight enough to put the kibosh on this robbery. I'll bet he can shoot straight enough when that door rolls back an' the Walker gang comes face to face with a bunch of Winchesters. Just prop him in a corner with a gun in his hand an' stay out of his way, Lou."

The engineer clamped a firm hand on Hogue's shoulder. "You civilians just wouldn't understand, Lou, but this here's a *railroadin'* man. They don't come no better than that."

The group moved together toward the waiting train. There was still work to be done, but Hogue did not doubt for a moment that it would all get done. A report had already been telegraphed to Pueblo. By now they would have quit making up the eastbound special, and that was probably the same engine they would use to haul a load of deputies and railroad security men out toward the siding. Not that there should be much for the special crew to do by the time they got there. By then the Walker gang should be dead or in irons, whichever way they preferred it.

Afterward, Hogue thought, well, he might take a few days off. He could use some time in town. Spend some of that money he had on the books. And maybe—he smiled to himself—maybe while he was there, after he bought himself a new crutch and some decent clothes, why maybe he just might drop by and pay a visit to Mrs. Cutcheon after all. It could not hurt. Could not hurt at all.

They reached the end of the platform, and Hogue hopped nimbly down into the gravel bed, using his single crutch for balance but getting along just fine. He liked it that no one felt it necessary to offer him any assistance. And he liked it too, he discovered, that the other men matched their pace to his as a matter of course. Oddly enough, he did not feel in the least embarrassed or upset about that. A week before, he probably would have.

And did you hear? Hogue asked himself. That engineer, Jake, had called him a railroadin' man. Now, any cowboy knows that that is not supposed to be any kind of a compliment. But still. . . . It was kind of nice anyway. Coming from a railroading man, that is. Let a cowhand say that to him and Hogue would punch the son of a buck. But from an engineer, well, it was not all that bad.

Hogue squared his shoulders as they reached the open door of the baggage car, where the safe and payroll were kept. He accepted a boost into the interior of the car and looked for a place he could sit near the door.

"Hand me that Winchester, boys, we got some work to do down the line. And don't none of you civilians get in my way, hear?" He gave the engineer a wink as the door was being slid shut against the outside world.

Hogue hurt like hell. His head was gashed open. He had bruises and pains over most of his body. His stump was still raw and sore from where Al had pressed live coals to it. There was not a muscle in his body that did not ache or pain him one way or another. Hogue Bynell felt just fine.